little lives

stories by
John Picard

D0916692

MINT HILL BOOKS
MAIN STREET RAG PUBLISHING COMPANY
CHARLOTTE, NORTH CAROLINA

Copyright © 2007, John Picard.

Cover photo by: David Smith-Soto

Acknowledgements:

Iowa Review: "Sinatra: A Memoir"
  (winner of the Tim McGinnis Award for humorous fiction)
The Crescent Review: "Guys"
The Greensboro Review: "Inga"
Rosebud: "The Stand-in"
West Branch: "Moving Away"
Mid-American Review: "Tics"
Kansas Quarterly: "Nimbus"
The Seattle Review: "Nixon: The Man And His Muse"

Library of Congress Control Number: 2007931000

ISBN 13: 978-1-59948-086-2

Produced in the United States of America

Mint Hill Books
Main Street Rag Publishing Company
PO Box 690100
Charlotte, NC 28227-7001
www.MainStreetRag.com

For Beth, Cathy, M.A., Mark, Patricia and Sarah

Our little life is rounded with a sleep

–William Shakespeare

Contents:

Sinatra: A Memoir

It's Frank's world.
We just live in it.
— Dean Martin

The caller, a raspy-voiced man, said a reservation had been made in my name for tomorrow's 9 a.m. flight out of Friendship Airport, landing in Las Vegas. I'd be staying at the Sands Hotel, courtesy of Frank Sinatra.

"But I have classes," I told him. "I'm not sure I can get someone to fill in for me on such short notice."

"He wants to see ya. Don't let 'im down. Frank doesn't like people what let 'im down."

"But why would he want to see me?"

"He read somethin' a yours."

It was 1959. I was an associate professor of Classics and Humanities at Johns Hopkins University (master's: Columbia; doctorate: Tulane), all three of my books had appeared in one of the better university presses, I had recently published an article in *Daedalus*, and only last year I'd been mentioned on page 7 of *The New York Times Book Review*. So I wasn't exactly unknown. "I'm honored, of course. I've long been a fan of his music. But I'm puzzled as to why–"

"Jus' get out here," the man said. "Some of the boys'll meet ya at the airport."

"Some of the boys?"

After landing, I was whisked from the terminal by two large yet swift-moving men who led me to a waiting limousine. Arriving at the hotel, flanked by my beefy escorts, I was taken up an elevator, then ushered into a beautifully appointed suite. My host was wearing a maroon smoking jacket with a black felt collar and "FAS" monogrammed on his lapel. A white handkerchief protruded from the breast pocket. Appropriately, he was smoking. (We all did then.) He was still thin, but no longer the scrawny crooner of his bobbysoxer days. His smile was utterly charming; his handshake was firm without being vise-like.

I told him how much I admired his recent work with Capitol Records, and he complimented me in turn on my latest monograph. "I dig what you said about the pre-Socratics," was how he put it.

He waved me into the living room area. "Get you anything to drink, Doc? Booze, beer, wine?"

"A little white wine might be nice."

He straddled a chair he'd dragged over from the dining room, a glass of Jack Daniels in one hand, a burning cigarette in the other. His fabled blue eyes appraised me intently. Then, without preamble, he began throwing out random ideas and observations, some quite complex and original, with references to thinkers both classical and modern. I was at a loss at first; I hadn't known this side of the superstar even existed. Before long, though, I was bouncing my own thoughts right back at him, and a kind of freewheeling exchange ensued. Over the course of the next hour we discussed, among other things, the major figures of the quattrocento, the causes of World War I, Wittgenstein's "picture theory," the decline of the Byzantine Empire, general relativity, Vico's *Scienza Nuova*, Freud's claim for Moses' Egyptian lineage, Zoroastrianism, and the narrative structure of *Bleak House*. He was equally knowledgeable on all these subjects. He had something fresh and new to say about each of them, and as I sipped an excellent Chardonnay, the conviction grew that I was in the presence of an extraordinary mind: a thinker, a polymath, a savant, an intellectual in the best sense of that word—in sum, one of the most impressive autodidacts it had ever been my privilege to meet.

I told him so.

He smiled, pleased, then got down to why he'd brought me there. He was interested in making me a part of his entourage, he said. He'd just finished a movie and he planned to start touring again later that month. He wanted me to go on the road with him.

I didn't know what to say.

He mentioned the salary. The figure was incredible.

I asked for a more detailed description of my duties, but apparently all that would be required was that I be available to spend time in his company.

"I need to think about this," I said. "I have a career, you know. I'm very well-respected in my field."

"Go on sabbatical. Apply for a research leave. Look, baby, I like what happened between us just now. I thought it was a gas."

We did seem to have a rapport, and it had been stimulating. Very different from the show-offy games of one-upsmanship my colleagues went in for. Here was intellection for its own sake, for the simple joy of it. I hadn't experienced anything like it since those old undergraduate bull sessions. "That's really all the job entails?" I said. "Hanging around? Talking to you?"

"That's it."

Besides a long and finally broken engagement, a couple of mild affairs, and a waning passion for contract bridge, there had been little else in my life apart from scholarly pursuits; certainly no adventures.

I stood up and put out my hand.

"Well, ring-a-ding-ding."

From the first stop on the tour I found myself summoned at all hours of the day and night. He would be pacing back and forth in his suite between shows or after an evening of heavy drinking or in the middle of an assignation. Invariably some of his lackeys would be present, the sharkskin-suited toughs who laughed at all his jokes, lit his cigarettes, procured female companionship; or some robed young woman sitting with her legs tucked under her, snapping her cigarette over an ashtray, glaring at the intruder. He would dismiss them with a wave. Often his first words to me would reflect a residual crudeness. "What is it with broads?" Or "Who the hell needs this screwy business?" But as we got onto some more elevated subject, most often a continuation of a previous discussion (the French Revolution, Tu Fu, Sputnik, Watteau–his interests were stunningly wide-ranging), a change would come over him. He would begin to lose his restlessness, stop his pacing and eventually light on some chair or sofa. After half an hour most traces of his profane, hipsterish speech would have vanished, replaced by an articulate and refined mode of expression–although never entirely. I remember poignantly, for instance, his referring to Robespierre as "one rebarbative cat." He was as mercurial in temperament as he was inquisitive of mind, and our time together often ended abruptly. As he rejoined his cronies it was not unusual to hear him utter some obscenity in greeting, his reversion well under way.

His singing had never been better. No matter what the city–San Francisco, Cleveland, Chicago–at the end of every performance the audience was on its feet, applauding, cheering, pleading for more. He'd lost a bit in the way of range and timbre. There were undoubtedly singers with better pipes around. But the Jack Joneses, the Buddy Grecos, let alone the myriad Avalons and Rydells, could not touch him for interpretation of lyrics, subtlety of phrasing, emotional nuance.

My sudden ascendancy to the inner circle met with mixed reactions. Unlike the more sinister elements of his entourage (the bodyguards, the professional goons and other unsavory types), who regarded me with suspicion, even contempt, Frank's swinging show business buddies–Sammy Davis, Jr., Joey Bishop, Dean Martin, Peter Lawford (known collectively as the Rat Pack)–gave me their complete support, accepted me totally. When I had some spare time and didn't feel like reading in my room, I would sometimes allow them to cajole me into a night of merrymaking. Though not themselves of an intellectual bent, they seemed to have grasped Frank's need for a brainy companion; also, I think they appreciated that I was capable of pulling him out of some of his darker moods, redirecting his sometimes irrational and destructive behavior.

I shall never forget the night at Villa Capri when he threw a plate of linguine into our waiter's face. (The pasta had arrived completely cooked, instead of al dente, the way Frank liked it.) Or the time he badly sprained his hand taking a swipe at a columnist who'd written of his underworld connections. I tried to be more attuned to his mood swings. At dinner soon after, following an argument at the bar between Frank and his latest love interest (Juliet or Lauren or Angie, I forget which), he returned to the table in the foulest of tempers. Normally I refrained from initiating intellectual repartee in front of the rest of the entourage. Not only would no one besides Frank and myself have been able to follow, but his sensitivity to his manly image precluded public discussions about the Ballet Russe, say, or the novels of the Brontes— which he adored, incidentally. But I decided this was an emergency and, sitting next to him (his teeth were gritted, his eyes a molten blue), I began luring him into a discussion of Leonardo's notebooks. We'd been marveling over a new leather bound edition of them just that morning. I said to him, "When Nietzsche wrote of the Vitruvian Man 'Stripped of myth, man stands famished among all his past'—don't you think he'd failed to take into account Leonardo's ambivalent humanism?" Immediately I could see the tension begin to drain from his face. In a matter of minutes, we were deep in conversation, the crisis averted.

He hadn't even graduated from high school, a fact of which he was much ashamed. (He had an inordinate respect for academic degrees, not uncommon among the undereducated, I've found.) I did my best to make him see that his shame was misplaced. I cited his fine analytical mind, the vast amount of reading he'd done on his own, and not least of all his rich lode of life experiences. But I had little success. It hadn't been until recently, after all, that he'd begun taking himself seriously as an intellect. Before enlisting me in his ranks he'd cocooned himself with performers, athletes, hoodlums, press agents, and sundry other hangers-on, none of whom possessed anything like his cerebral concerns, his mental rigor. How miserable, how frustrated, he must have been during that time: so many thoughts and no one to share them with. It helped explain, perhaps as much as his difficulties with Ava, the uniquely high quality of those Capitol recordings of the mid and late fifties, the pathos and pain that came through with every note, the honest suffering transmuted on such classic albums as "No One Cares," "Only the Lonely," "Where Are You?"

The aura of being around such famous people was bound to rub off and I found myself attracting beautiful and glamorous women. Most of these, I knew, were only trying to get close to Frank, but failing that, close to someone who was close to Frank. During our Atlantic City engagement, it struck me that I'd had more women in my bed over the last two days than I'd had in all of my previous life.

I was the beneficiary of his legendary largess. In addition to cases of premium wines, he gifted me with theater tickets, watches, pinkie rings, television sets, and, gem of gems, the 1911 Britannica. His respect for the life of the mind did not extend to its traditional disregard for appearances. He accused me of dressing like a clyde: in Pack-ese, a square. He insisted I accompany him on a clothes-buying spree, his mere presence creating pandemonium in half a dozen of Manhattan's finest stores that day. He was a dapper and meticulous dresser himself and, under his personal supervision, I traded in my tweeds and loafers for a couple of the three hundred dollar sharkskin suits he favored, a dozen silk ties, and as many pairs of custom-made English shoes. We made one last stop at a jewelry store where he bought me a gold plated cigarette case. I still have this. The inscription reads: To Doc. Think lovely thoughts. Frank.

In Detroit one sizzling afternoon, while we were down by the hotel pool (discussing neo-Confucianism, I think it was), his valet came by and urged us to join him and some other staff members in a game of poker. Frank said he wasn't interested; I said I was. When he realized I was thinking of going without him we got into quite a little tiff over it. I did not like him shouting at me and told him so. I also didn't appreciate my towel and things being thrown into the deep end. He apologized and we wound up going to the game together. But it was the first indication I had that he was becoming overly dependent on me.

I had the clothes. I was picking up the lingo. I was seldom more than a highball behind Dino who, interestingly, could not hold his liquor. (Sammy and I hauled him back to his room on numerous occasions.) I become, in short, an unofficial member of the Rat Pack. I prowled the night clubs and the casinos with them, chased women with them, got into trouble with them. In Cincinnati we stole a bread truck at 2 a.m. and roared around town, hanging out the doors and shouting at passersby, until Frank drove it through a grocery's plate glass window. Only his offer to defray the cost of all the damages, and then some, kept it out of the papers.

It was as if I had become a part of the boyhood gang from which I had always been excluded, my bookish ways alienating me from my coevals, making me either an object of ridicule (four eyes) or one of exaggerated and ironic respect (brain). In consequence I had never before experienced the camaraderie of my own sex, seeing in all groups of men a shallow and juvenile fellowship at best, a conspiracy to brutalize at worst. But without knowing it I had always yearned for such company; the former, that is.

Around this time he said of the Rat Pack, "They're good for a few laughs and some dirty jokes, but let's face it, that's about it."

"That's a lot, though," I protested. "You take it for granted, Frank, but most middle-aged men don't even have friends."

"But their view of things–it's so narrow."

"They're great guys."

"Yeah, but I can't talk to them, not the way I can talk to you. They lack depth."

My peculiar status was frequently the object of the Pack's habitual bantering. There was none of the maliciousness I'd suffered as a boy, however. Instead, their ribbing was a sign of affection, a source of fraternal humor like Frank's mob ties, Sammy's race, Joey's Jewishness, Dean's drinking, Peter's in-laws. I relished their jibes.

"I didn't think you'd dig the guys this much," Frank said. "I thought you'd remain, well, more aloof–considering your background, your education."

He had a romanticized view of the intellectual life.

"That doesn't mean I can't have fun. You enjoy yourself with them."

"That's different." He looked away and said with a mirthless laugh, "Dean doesn't even know what century the Civil War took place in."

"So?"

"Sam thinks Rabelais is a type of cheese."

"They have other qualities, Frank."

"They call you egg-head, bookworm, pencil-neck..."

"I'm well aware of that."

Then I understood. He was jealous. He was jealous of my relationship with his friends.

I had just returned to my room early one morning when the phone started ringing. I knew it was him, but I was expecting a visitor (a russet-haired former Miss Texas, now a lounge hostess) and even if I hadn't been, I probably wouldn't have answered it. I'd had enough for one day. When he wasn't summoning me to a late night confab, he was collaring me when I was chatting up some show girl, or bending my ear throughout dinner, or following me into the john (this actually happened), all in order to raise some obscure philosophical point. I suppose I was feeling stifled. I enjoyed our talks as much as ever, but I needed a break once in a while, something I'm not sure he ever understood. And perhaps I was growing a little tired of his seeing me one dimensionally, as a mind and nothing else. He never asked me a personal question, or inquired about my health, or appeared to care one way or another about my deeper feelings.

"Maybe you'd better lay off the booze a little," he said.

I'd just served myself three fingers of Jack Daniels.

"Lay off the booze? Baby, what do you mean?"

Stroking his chin, he said, "Nothing. Just slow down. Just take it easy." He looked at me. "You didn't even notice, did you?"

"Notice what, Frank?"

He drew a breath. "You said Giotto when you meant Cimabue just now."

"Did I?"

"Yeah, you did."

We'd been talking about the early Renaissance masters. The Leonardo books had piqued his interest. "Common mistake," I said.

"I guess." Then, "Why don't you get some rest and come back later? We'll take up where we left off."

I fully intended to return, but I ran into Dean in the lobby and we ended up willy-nilly at the local track. Frank reached me in my room hours later. He was irate. I told him I'd forgotten, and I had. The crash I heard was the phone smashing against his bedroom wall. We avoided each other for a few days, then he sent me a signed copy of Margaret Mead's latest book, as a sort of apology or peace offering, or both, plus an invitation to meet him after that night's performance. It was one of our longest sessions ever, lasting until dawn, but there was something desperate about it, forced, as if we were fanning a dying flame.

Then it was back to Vegas.

I'd been looking forward to it since the tour began: a Summit Meeting, a gathering of the whole clan for a week of performances in the Copa room at the Sands, with all the on-stage drinking and cutting-up, the tossing of cream pies in the hotel's steamroom, the round-the-clock swinging, all the things I'd heard about that made it such an event.

Unfortunately, he seemed to have more need of me during these frenetic, fun-filled days than at any other time in our travels. He wanted me backstage before he went on, right down front during the show, and close at hand afterwards, trooping with him from party to party, bar to bar. This was true even when it wasn't appropriate, when he had some woman in tow who was clearly uncomfortable with me there, not to mention the high-toned conversation from which she was cavalierly excluded.

After the second show on Saturday, Sammy and Peter and I decided to catch the Ink Spots at the Dunes. I'd gone back to my room for a change of clothes when the phone rang. Without thinking I picked it up. Frank wanted to see me right away.

"Can't it wait, baby?"

"No, it can't wait–*baby*."

When I got there he was pacing between the picture window and the dining room. His unshaven face was drawn and pale; his eyes were bloodshot. Physically he was exhausted; intellectually it was another story.

"Great show tonight."

He mumbled his thanks.

John Picard

I headed over to the bar. "Mind if I help myself to some Jackie D?"

"Haven't you had enough for one–?" He waved his hand dismissively, then resumed his pacing, snapping his fingers as if to get his mind revved. He could go on for hours, I thought despairingly. "I've been thinking about something," he began. "I've got my own ideas, but I'm curious to know what you have to say. What do you think he meant when he wrote, 'Only when love is a duty, only then is love eternally secure?'"

"What who wrote?"

He stopped in his tracks. "Who?"

I checked my watch.

"It sounds familiar."

"It sounds familiar. It *sounds* familiar? You don't recognize a quote from Kierkegaard?" He was yelling, and yet there was something plaintive underneath his angry words. "You wrote a book on Kierkegaard."

"He was one of my sources, he wasn't–"

He raised a hand. "Forget it, OK? Forget it."

"I'm just tired, baby. And besides, who cares?"

I was sure I saw him flinch. There was a long silence as he shuffled over to the big arm chair in front of the window. He sat with his cigarette cupped in his hand the way he did when he was pensive.

"Is it all right if I split now?" I yawned loudly.

After a moment, "Sure. Split."

I let myself out of the suite.

The next morning I couldn't open the door to my room. The lock had been changed. The front desk refused to give me a key. They said they were under strict orders not to; I didn't have to ask from whom. There was a plane ticket and all my things packed in the three-piece luggage set Frank had given me last month for my 39th birthday.

I had to find him. Hurrying through the lobby, I came upon Sammy at the slot machines. He told me Frank had found out where we'd been last night. When it became clear I'd lied to him he stormed through the hotel, broke into my room and tore it apart. "If I were you, Doc, I'd stay away. I've never seen him like this."

I thanked Sammy for his concern, but I was certain I could entice him out of his bad mood, as I'd done so often before.

He was in the casino, surrounded at the craps table by virtually the entire entourage. "Frank," I called to him.

Joey and Dean and Peter glanced anxiously from me to their leader.

He tossed the dice. Snake eyes.

"Frank, I–"

"Get this creep out of my sight."

Two of his goons grabbed my arms and started dragging me toward the exit. Kicking, squirming, I repeatedly hollered his name.

"Wait," he said. He swaggered over, puffing on a cigarette.

I was sweating profusely. I could smell alcohol seeping through my pores. The goons tightened their hold on me. "Can't we talk about this, Frank? How about getting together later? I've been thinking about what you said. For Kierkegaard, the duty to love is a paradox, one of Christianity's hard sayings, if you will, which–"

"It's too late for that," he barked and made a sideways chopping motion. It was the exact same one he used on stage, if much less crisply, during the first crescendo of "I'll Never Smile Again." He stepped closer to me. "It's over. You're all through. You dig?"

"But why, Frank? Why?"

He sucked on his cigarette, then removed it from his lips. Smoke dribbled out of one corner of his mouth. "Because baby, you're just not intelligent anymore."

I did my best to maintain contact with Sammy and the others, but they weren't big on letter-writing, nor did they always return my calls. I asked each of them to intercede for me with Frank, but they said he wouldn't even discuss it, that the mere mention of my name sent him into a rage. This gave me hope, made me think he still might care.

The university had taken me back, once my case had gone before a review committee. My research leave had been limited to only one semester and I'd been AWOL for weeks. It was a tough adjustment for me. I'd been leading a very different kind of existence, and my colleagues seemed such a dull lot.

I followed the Pack's activities in the media, but this only whetted my appetite for my old life. I couldn't afford to fly all over the country, but I did manage a trip to Vegas that summer; another Summit Meeting. The guys were extremely busy, of course, and it wasn't easy for them to get together with me. (I was still barred from the Sands.) But we did finally meet for a drink at a bar on the strip, on the fourth and final day of my visit.

It did not go well. The drinks were watery, everyone was hung over, and worst of all, we had nothing to say to each other. We never had. I think we were relieved whenever somebody came by our table to ask for an autograph.

All at once their limitations became glaringly obvious to me. I knew then it wasn't the Pack I'd been missing. It was him. I missed Frank. I missed our talks. I recalled that just before our break we'd had numerous discussions about the Stoics. (Frank couldn't get enough of Epictetus and committed whole sections of the *Enchiridion* to memory.) They intrigued him, I now realized, because they advocated what he himself was striving for, the ability to enjoy the fruits of one's success without becoming a slave to them. "So how is he?" I said.

Everyone sort of muttered and stared into their drinks.

"What is it?" I said. "What's happened?"

"You'd probably find out sooner or later," Sammy said.

"Find out what?"

"He's got someone new."

"Someone new? You mean...?"

Sammy just nodded.

"Who?"

He didn't recall his name. Neither did Joey or Peter who said, "He's a real clyde. I don't know what Frank sees in him."

Dean said, "Boris something. Ascow. Blascow. I don't talk to the guy, myself."

"He doesn't dig us the way you did," Sammy added, graciously.

"Boris Glasgow?" I said. "Dr. Boris Glasgow?"

"That's him. That's the cat."

He was a good man, I had to admit. Glasgow, whom I'd heard give a paper some time back at the MLA in Washington, was the Lopes Professor of Art, History and Urban Affairs at the University of Southern California. Only forty-five and at the top his field, he had an international reputation, had published book after book (with Scribners, no less), and had once appeared on Jack Paar as some sort of expert on cultural trends.

"Well, that's that, isn't it?" I said.

"Sorry, Doc," Joey said.

"Yeah, sorry," the others echoed.

"Well, thanks for coming," I told them. "It's been great, but...maybe you better go now." I didn't want them to see how upset I was, and they were in a hurry to get back anyway.

I walked them outside to their limousine.

I shook hands with Joey and Peter.

"Not the same without you, pally," Dean said, clapping me on the shoulder.

Sammy gave me a hug. "Ciao, baby. And stay in touch."

None of it was real. We knew we'd never see one another again.

After watching the limo slip into traffic, I got in my rental and sped away. I tried to draw comfort from another great Stoic, Marcus Aurelius, who writes in book six of the *Meditations*, "The pain which is intolerable carries us off; but that which lasts a long time is tolerable." I drove out of the city and kept going. Soon I was cruising in the desert. After a while I began to sing. It wasn't something I normally did–I haven't much of a voice–but the mood was on me. I was singing one of those piercing, mournful ballads he'd recorded a few years back. When I got to the end of it, I started singing another one, and after that, another. Driving through the desert that night so long ago, I sang every sad song of his I could remember, and I remembered quite a few.

Guys

Friday morning Baxter went down to the reproduction room to make copies of his petty cash records. Williams, director of public relations, was standing at the machine. "Almost done," he said.

Leaning against the doorway, Baxter crossed his long legs and rested his chin in his hand. It was his third week on the job and he still hadn't struck up an acquaintance with any of his new co-workers. He tried now to think of something to say to Williams, some bit of small talk. "How's the copy quality on those?"

Williams picked up one of his copies and scrutinized it. "Fine."

"I had the service man in yesterday. I just wondered."

"Looks good to me." Williams began to smile. "Thought of you on the way to work this morning, Baxter. No rain in the forecast, yet there I am on K

Street, caught in a downpour with no umbrella. You had yours, I bet."

"Oh, yes." Baxter always carried his umbrella to work with him, no matter what the forecast. It surprised him that Williams had noticed. "Used to be," he said, "the only time I got wet was when it wasn't going to rain."

Williams chuckled. "My wife's always trying to get me to wear galoshes, always trying to sneak them into my briefcase. I sure wish I had them this morning."

"It's just the opposite with me. I'm the one trying to get my wife to dress properly. Elizabeth buys all these beautiful dresses, then she won't wear anything over them, any sort of wrap. Even when it's freezing out."

Williams was staring at him. "You're married?"

"Why, yes."

"I didn't know."

Baxter had been telling people he was married for some time now. At his age, forty-two, being single was an embarrassment, more so every day. To say to people, "I'm a bachelor," seemed to elicit only suspicious looks and wry smiles. Being married made everything easier.

"My wife's name is Felice," Williams said. "You know what Felice means, don't you?"

"I'm not sure I do."

"Happiness. I see you don't wear a ring."

"I, I've never gone in for that sort of thing," Baxter said, and immediately noticed the gold band on

William's finger. "I mean, it's all right for other people. I suppose I have simple tastes."

"Kind of a purist."

"You might say that, yes."

Williams gathered up his copies and smiled. "Nice talking to you, Baxter."

"Nice talking to you."

Later that day, a few minutes after six, he heard a loud knock on his door. "Yes?"

It was Williams. "Burning the midnight oil, eh?"

"I just have some accounts I need to catch up on." Baxter slid open a drawer and dropped in his paperback.

Williams said he was on his way to meet the guys from legal at the Ha' Penny Lion. The Bullets' game was being shown on a wide screen and he wondered if Baxter would like to join them. "If you're not too busy."

Baxter stroked his chin. "Sure. Why not?" Thrilled, he turned off his PC and threw on his sports coat.

"Don't you have to call your wife first?" Williams said. "It could be a late night."

"Right. Thanks for reminding me."

Williams stepped into the corridor but the door was ajar; he was well within earshot.

Baxter dialed the weather. "It's me. Um, I've been invited to watch the basketball game at one of the bars around here, so I won't be home for a while." He paused. "No. Don't wait up...Just some people from the office...Uh-huh..." He paused again. "I'm not sure exactly. Eleven–eleven-thirty...You sure you don't mind?...All right then. Bye." Suddenly inspired, he added, "I love you, too," and hung up.

"Elizabeth take it okay?"

"No problem."

"I don't know about you two, but Felice and I make it a habit to be with our own friends. About once a month. This is her bridge night."

Baxter wiped his sweating palms on his pants leg. "A wise policy, I'm sure."

"We find it feeds the marriage."

They walked up 17th Street and cut across to L. It felt good to be out on the town for a change.

It made Baxter think his decision to find a new job (the same job, really–office manager with bookkeeping duties) had been a good one after all. He'd been having his doubts about it lately, for he'd fallen into his old pattern of staying late at the office whether or not he had work to do. Anything to postpone his departure for home. If he arrived there before seven, he'd found, the evening stretched out interminably. His apartment needed only so much straightening. He'd never cared for television, and movies weren't much to his taste either. He'd once been an avid theatergoer, taking in shows at the National Theater and the Kennedy Center, but he could no longer find anyone to accompany him and he didn't like going alone. At one time he'd had a lot hobbies to occupy him: coin collecting, photography, tennis. Then there was the year he tried graduate school, but he'd lost his enthusiasm for that too.

When they arrived at the Ha' Penny Lion, Williams rushed ahead to open the door for him. Stocky, about a foot shorter than Baxter, he had a big head and thinning blond hair. Baxter felt a sudden affection for this man who'd pulled him out of his solitude and, stepping inside, he said, "Thanks so much," imbuing his words with what he hoped was a special warmth.

The others had grabbed a table near the back of the crowded bar. Baxter was trying to find a place to put his umbrella when Charnoff, the Association's Capitol Hill lobbyist, asked, "Do you ever go anywhere without that?"

Kirkland, Charnoff's legislative assistant, said, "I've wanted to ask that myself."

Apparently everyone had noticed. "I try not to," he said and hooked it on the back of his chair.

"I'm just curious," Charnoff said. "Don't get me wrong. I admire a man who stands by his eccentricities." Charnoff was a large man with a perpetual five o'clock shadow. Kirkland, also dark and hairy, seemed a slightly trimmer version of his boss. Like Baxter, they were all in their forties. Charnoff went to the bar and came back with a fresh pitcher of beer and a plate of chicken wings.

The game started. Baxter wasn't a basketball fan, but he followed the action closely, expressing dismay every time the Bullet's faltered, excitement whenever they were racking up points, which was often. By the end of the second quarter everyone was muttering blow-out.

Kirkland bought the next pitcher. Beer wasn't Baxter's beverage of choice, or at least so much of it, but in the interest of group solidarity, he matched the other men mug for mug.

Charnoff wagged his cigarette a la Groucho Marx. "Home in on that action, gentleman." He indicated a shapely brunette stepping across the room, snug in a black leather skirt.

Kirkland turned a hundred and eighty degrees in his chair. "Ouch."

She wasn't Baxter's type but he chimed in anyway, "Very nice."

Only Williams remained focused on the big-screen TV.

Charnoff leaned over the table. "You mean you won't even look? Not one little peek? We won't tell. I promise."

Williams took a sip of beer.

"We all look."

"Not Williams," Kirkland said. "Other women don't exist for him."

"I refuse to believe that," Charnoff said. "It's too depressing."

"They always tease me about Felice," Williams explained to Baxter.

"It's for his own good."

"They think it's foolish, a husband devoted to his wife."

"Who's not devoted?" Charnoff said. "We're all devoted. What concerns us"–he dragged on his cigarette–"What concerns us is his indifference to feminine pulchritude."

"His what?" Kirkland said.

"His limp dick."

Everyone laughed, no one harder than Williams.

"Check this out." Kirkland said, leering at a blonde in tight-fitting jeans, her black pumps clicking over the wood floor.

Charnoff turned to Baxter. "I guess you think we're pretty pathetic, married men lusting after young flesh."

"Baxter's married," Williams said.

Charnoff looked at Baxter. "I was sure you were a bachelor. Beg your pardon."

Kirkland jabbed Charnoff in the ribs. "By the bar. My God! She's got the–"

"That's enough," Charnoff said abruptly. "Williams is right. Hell, none of these women have anything on Carla. They're young, sure, but that's all they are."

"What's wrong with young?" Kirkland said.

"I'd put Carla up against any woman here. I mean that."

"That's like what I was telling Felice the other night," Williams said. "She thinks she's getting old, and I guess she is. I mean, who isn't? But it looks great on her. I love her wrinkles."

"Carla's been graying for some time now. Prematurely. I don't know how often I've told her not to put that damn rinse in her hair. She's afraid I'm losing interest, I guess, which is nuts. You know what Carla's best feature is? They say you can tell a person's age by their hands. Well, Carla's got the hands of a teenager."

Kirkland said, "Gail's got the same legs she's always had. Firm and shapely. The kind that look great in heels. Men still stare at her in the street. I've seen them."

Baxter was about to say something but Kirkland broke in, insisting that Williams buy another plate of chicken wings, and the opportunity was lost. He saw then it was his turn to do the honors and, picking up the empty pitcher, started for the bar.

"Aren't you forgetting something?" Charnoff called after him. He waited for Baxter to come all the way back to the table, then handed him his umbrella. Everyone cracked up. Baxter, who remembered what a good sport Williams had been, joined in the laughter. This proved to be the correct response. "You're all right, Baxter," Charnoff told him and clapped him several times on the arm.

It was three deep at the bar. He waited among the K Street corridor types, youngish men and women, drinking and talking and flirting. Once he used to frequent bars of this sort, singles hang-outs, only they weren't called that then. He would drive down on a Friday or Saturday night and go from one to the next, hoping to meet someone.

He was not unhandsome. He was on the thin side and he stooped a little, but his hair was dark and wavy and he had deep-set eyes with long lashes and a chin with the hint of a cleft. Even his one flaw, his tiny wing-like ears, did not detract much from his looks. Yet it had been years since he dated anyone, not since he and Elizabeth had been an item.

At the time he'd thought of her as a potential fiancee. One evening shortly before these hopes were dashed he'd looked on in confusion as she launched into a strange pantomime. Thrusting her hand into an imaginary pocket, she stared off with a look of exaggerated self-possession, like an aristocrat scanning a drawing room. Then, moving stiffly on her sinewy legs to the other side of his little apartment, she put her feet together and stood with her arms over her chest, chin upraised. Next she put her hands behind her back and assumed an at-ease posture. It was then he realized she was imitating him. "You're always posing," she said, not meanly; perhaps, even, with a touch of sympathy. "Everything you do is thought out and preplanned."

"I wasn't aware of that actually."

"Even the way you talk."

When he got back to the bar, Kirkland was saying, "I'm always bitching and moaning, but Gail's got it much tougher. I do what I can, you know, but she's their mother. Kids want to be with their mother. After working all day, she fixes dinner, and I'm not talking Swanson's frozen dinners either. These are gourmet meals. Beef burgundy and shrimp creole and shit. Incredible. She's too damn good for me is what I'm saying, I guess."

"Yeah," Charnoff said, "I know what you mean. I don't know what I ever did to deserve Carla. I swear to God I don't. I'm not the easiest guy to live with. I'm not what you'd call the sensitive type."

Kirkland laughed. "You got that right."

Charnoff glared across the table. "I'm serious."

"Sorry," Kirkland said.

"Carla puts up with a lot. I'm the first to admit it. Never complains, though. Not a peep out of her. Woman are the real stoics, not men. Look at us: nothing but a bunch of babies. We get a little head cold and we think it's the end of the world. We think it's important. We whine and whine. Not women. They just go on. They take it all in stride." He puffed on his cigarette. "I did a really crappy thing last week. I still feel bad about it. I'm surprised Carla's even speaking to me." He fell silent.

"What did you do?"

Charnoff looked around the table, then he said, "I forgot her birthday. Can you believe that? Can you believe forgetting your wife's one and only thirty-fifth birthday?" There were actual tears in Charnoff's eyes.

"What a piece-a-shit thing to do to someone." He jammed his cigarette in the ashtray, flipping it over.

Kirkland placed a consoling hand on his shoulder. "Easy, guy."

Charnoff passed his hand over his eyes. "I'm all right." He looked at Williams. "I bet you never forget your wife's birthday."

"February fourteenth."

"Valentine's Day, for Christ's sake."

"Felice loves double features, a thing from her childhood. So we always see two movies that day, with a meal at the restaurant of her choice between shows."

"That's a swell thing to do," Kirkland said. "I never take Gail anywhere, even on her goddamn birthday. That's the kind of guy I am."

"A rat," Charnoff said. "We're all rats–except for Williams."

Baxter, determined not to miss out this time, blurted, "I took Elizabeth to the Kennedy Center–on her birthday. It was right before Christmas and I bought tickets to The Nutcracker. Elizabeth studied ballet for ten years. She could have been a soloist if she'd stuck with it. After the ballet we went to Chez Camille, the French place off Connecticut Avenue. We had filet mignon and white asparagus and Caesar salads. Elizabeth spoke French to the waiter the whole night. In the middle of dinner a man came into the restaurant selling roses. Long-stem red roses. He went from table to table, trying to get the men to buy a flower for their wives or girlfriends–their sweethearts, as he called them. You know how they do. The roses looked puny to me, but he was doing a brisk business. I'd already decided I wasn't going to buy one. My birthday present to Elizabeth had been the ballet and this great meal. Much more impressive gifts than an overpriced little rose, I thought. So when the man got to our table I just shook my head and he moved on. I went back to my steak. But later on I noticed that Elizabeth had gotten quiet. The birthday blues, I decided. But now I don't think so."

"You fucked up," Charnoff said.

"I believe I did, yes."

"You failed to meet the moment. That kind of thing means a lot to a woman. You're as bad as the rest of us."

"After dinner, to lift her spirits, I took her to the Ritz Carlton for drinks. We ordered champagne. Elizabeth did. She always chose–chooses the wine for us. She's something of a connoisseur that way."

"She sounds like quite the cosmopolitan, your wife," Charnoff said. "Quite the sophisticated lady."

"She is."

"So what's she doing with a bum like you?"

"I've often asked myself that. I've often wondered."

The check came. Baxter didn't want to leave, he'd just started to enjoy himself, but Charnoff was pretty loaded and Kirkland and Williams were eager to go.

The Metro had stopped running and Kirkland, the only one with a car, volunteered to drive everyone home.

They'd barely gotten under way when Charnoff, sitting beside Baxter in the back seat, suggested having a nightcap at Fred's, some joint a mile before the Maryland line. Baxter said one wouldn't hurt but the other two men were adamant about getting home. Then Charnoff started in about his desperate need for a vacation. They'd been running him ragged lately, he said. He couldn't wait to get to the Jersey shore where he had a cabin, a wedding present from his father-in-law. He was planning a trip there as soon as it turned warm. They were all invited. He wanted them and their wives to stay with him and Carla at the cabin in the spring.

"This isn't the booze talking either. I mean it. We've got tennis courts, a swimming pool, and all kinds of rooms. What do you say?"

Williams had to discuss it with Felice first, but it sounded good to him. Kirkland said he'd definitely consider it.

"What about you, Baxter? You and Elizabeth make it?"

He hadn't been to the beach since he was a boy. He didn't know why he'd allowed this to happen. He'd always loved playing in the waves. His parents had to beg him to get out of the water.

"Jesus!" Williams hit his fist against the dash. "What time is it?"

"About twelve-thirty," Kirkland said.

"I can't believe I did this."

"Did what?"

"We have this rule: if either of us is going to be later than midnight we always call–no matter what. Anyone got a cell? I left mine at the office."

Kirland handed his cell phone over the seat, but for some reason Williams couldn't get a signal. Charnoff didn't have his phone either and Baxter didn't own one.

"You can forget about finding a phone booth around here," Kirkland said. In Maryland now, they were entering a residential area.

"I'm surprised at you, Williams," Charnoff intoned. "The insensitivity this implies, the lack of caring. You, of all people."

"It completely slipped my mind."

"Yes, gentlemen, we're one bunch of undeserving sons-of-bitches."

"Hey, I know," Kirkland said. "Why don't you call from Baxter's. We're almost there."

"That all right with you, Baxter? I'd really appreciate it."

"Fine," he said. Then, "No, that won't work. Our phone's in the bedroom, and Elizabeth tends to turn in rather early, I'm afraid."

"I wouldn't want to disturb your wife," Williams said.

Charnoff draped an arm behind Baxter's shoulders, fingertips brushing his coat sleeve. His breath was foul and it was all Baxter could do not to turn away. "Do me a favor, will you? See what you can do about getting Elizabeth to come to the cabin. She sounds like Carla's type, cultured and all. We're always on the look-out for new couples."

"I promise I'll speak with her."

"We'll be hurt if she doesn't come. Tell her that."

"I will. But if she can't make it for some reason, I'd be happy to come by myself. We sometimes take separate vacations."

Charnoff gave him a bleary-eyed stare and patted his shoulder. "You're all right, Baxter," he said. "You're weird as hell, but you're all right."

Charnoff's words stung him. He would have liked to ask what he meant by calling him that, but this wasn't the place. Instead, he delivered the little speech he'd worked up.

"I want you all to know what a good time I've had this evening. Thanks so much for having me along. I hope we can do it again very soon....That's mine with the light on."

Kirkland stopped the car.

Baxter wished them all good night and, slipping out from under Charnoff's arm, stepped from the car. He'd reached the sidewalk when he saw Charnoff coming toward him with his umbrella. Stupidly, he'd left it on the seat. Moving swiftly if unsteadily, Charnoff looked delighted to be seeing him again so soon, as if he savored this unexpected meeting before being made to part. At the end of an energetic stride his foot struck the curb and he began to fall forward, arms flapping. He avoided landing just long enough to clear the grass and hit the sidewalk with his head. Baxter had run hard to catch him but arrived too late. He was trying to lift him by his shoulders when Williams and Kirkland appeared and together they got Charnoff to his feet.

"Christ," Kirkland said.

Blood was trickling down Charnoff's forehead.

"He's really hurt," Williams said. "Think we should get him to a doctor?"

"I'm okay," Charnoff said and grabbed his head.

"We should get him cleaned up, at least."

"Bring him inside," Baxter said. He'd gotten all the way to the door of his first floor apartment when he remembered. He hesitated, the key already in the lock.

"What's the hold-up?" Kirkland said.

Charnoff moaned behind him.

"What's the problem? We've got an injured man here."

"No problem," Baxter said, opened the door and flipped on the overhead. He directed them to the bathroom which was just inside the entrance.

John Picard

Kirkland and Williams lowered Charnoff onto the toilet seat. Baxter fetched some towels from the closet and gave them to Kirkland who ran one under warm water and dabbed at the wound. After cleaning off the blood, he pressed a damp wash cloth to Charnoff's forehead.

"Not so hard, damn it." Charnoff leaned his head back against the wall like a kid with a nose bleed.

"So how is he?"

"He's got a nasty bump but no cuts or anything. You in much pain?"

"Of course I'm in pain. I'm in terrible pain." Then he grumbled, "Hell, I'm all right."

"You got some aspirins or something I can give him, Baxter?"

Baxter got down the bottle of Advil from the medicine cabinet, then headed for the kitchen. This necessitated walking the length of the apartment, which had the effect of pulling Williams into the room. He was stepping onto the throw rug as Baxter returned with a water glass.

"There's a phone in here," Williams said, pointing at the end table with Baxter's umbrella.

"Yes."

"But you said..."

"Help yourself. Please."

Williams handed him the umbrella.

"Thanks so much."

Williams plopped down on the love seat and began dialing. Baxter continued on to the bathroom. When he heard Williams hang up, he wandered back in. "I was right. She was worried sick. God, I feel terrible now."

"You shouldn't, really. These things happen."

Williams stood up. "I almost forgot. I hope we didn't wake Elizabeth." His voice was lowered.

"Don't worry about that."

"Say, where's the bedroom in this place?"

Baxter forced a grin.

Williams proceeded to take in the apartment, the leather recliner–the only chair in the living room area–the little round table with one straight back chair pushed under it, the single bed in the corner. Williams stepped over and peeked in the kitchen. "This is an efficiency."

If there was some lie or bit of subterfuge that would have saved him, Baxter was unable to think of it. "Yes."

"You live alone."

Baxter nodded.

"I don't get it."

He gave a little shrug.

"Aren't you married?"

"Not actually."

Williams stared. "Not actually? But I heard you talking to your wife on the phone. At the office, remember?"

Baxter said nothing.

"That was her, wasn't it? You said it was."

"I did, yes. I apologize."

"So–Jesus–you mean you faked that?"

"I meant no harm."

Williams glanced away, as if trying to collect his thoughts, then looked at Baxter again. "But you did that?"

"Yes."

"Did you make everything else up too?"

"I made nothing up. Everything I said was true."

"Except that you don't have a wife."

"Except for that."

Williams started back across the room. Kirkland walked in and they almost collided.

"What's Charnoff doing?" Williams asked.

"Taking a leak." Kirkland patted the arm of the love seat. "Nice place you got here, Baxter." Frowning suddenly, he looked around him.

"There isn't one," Williams said.

"Huh?"

"There's no bedroom. That's the kitchen." Kirkland turned to Williams for further explanation. Williams whispered something into Kirkland's ear.

"What?" Kirkland said, incredulous.

Baxter gripped the umbrella handle so tight his knuckles ached. He hated the way the two men were looking at him. "I'm sorry I deceived you," he said.

Kirkland rolled his eyes.

Just then Charnoff came out of the bathroom holding a wash cloth to his head. "How about a nightcap? I think we've earned one. I know I have. You got anything to drink, Baxter?"

"We're leaving," Williams told him. "Now."

"I have some sherry," Baxter said.

Kirkland snickered and shook his head.

Charnoff wanted to know what was so funny.

"You wouldn't believe it." Kirkland opened the door and grabbed Charnoff by the elbow.

"Hey," he protested.

Williams got on Charnoff's other side.

"I'll see you all Monday morning," Baxter said, making one last attempt at amiability.

"Sorry I missed your wife," Charnoff said over his shoulder. "Don't forget about the cabin. Sometime in June."

"I won't."

Kirkland and Williams hustled Charnoff out the door and moved quickly down the sidewalk.

Baxter called after them, "I'm completely normal, I assure you."

The Stand-in

He is discovered while working as an extra in *The Day of the Locust*. A casting agent who happens to be on the set pulls him aside and asks if he'd like to be in Duncan Avery's next movie. Here it is, Michael thinks. The big break. At 44, he was beginning to wonder if it would ever happen. The casting agent explains that he is looking for a stand-in for Mr. Avery to whom he bears a striking physical resemblance. Has he heard this before? He allows that he has, quite often. He signs a contract that very evening and, the following week, flies to Charleston, South Carolina where the filming of *Jalopy Joe* is just getting underway.

He appears on screen a total of 17 times, mostly in a crash helmet. There are a dozen shots of him climbing in and out of beat-up old cars, several more of him huddling with some extras over a smoking engine. Duncan himself is all set to do one scene when it's decided it plays better from a distance and thus a stand-in will do just as well. In what turns out to be his longest scene in the movie, nearly three seconds, Michael places some coins in a vending machine and then kicks it.

Duncan Avery insists that he call him Dunc, everyone else does. Michael experiences from close up the legendary smile: "part Tweetie Bird, part Sylvester Cat, part street urchin, part riverboat gambler," as *Time* described it in a recent issue. But in subsequent meetings the famous actor is standoffish and formal, despite his immense charm. Initially Michael thinks it's a question of contrasting personalities and life-styles. Duncan Avery is garrulous and extroverted; Michael is a loner with few friends. The actor is seldom without a starlet on his arm; the stand-in is often unsure of himself in intimate situations. The actor's life is a tabloid tale of wild parties and high living; the stand-in spends most of his nights in, either reading or watching TV. They have little in common. Nevertheless, Michael hopes that Duncan (he cannot bring himself to say Dunc) will take him under his wing, serve as his mentor. Working up his courage one day, he asks the actor if he can arrange a screen test for him. Duncan is graciousness itself, agreeing to look into the matter at his earliest convenience. But nothing ever comes of it.

"When I first got this job," Sandy, another stand-in, tells him, "I was always hounding Clint about getting me this and that part, I used to be a pretty fair character actor, you know. 'Sure thing, Sandy,' he'd say. 'I'll see what I can do, Sandy.'"

"And what happened?"

"Nothing."

"Didn't that bother you?"

"Naw. Oh, at first. But I know he meant well."

"He broke his promise."

"Not really. He just never got around to it. They're very busy men. They don't always have time for such things."

He was christened Michael Lambert Smith. When he was starting out in dinner theater he spent a lot of time trying to decide on a professional moniker. He wanted something memorable that also retained the flavor of his given name. Having observed that an unusual first name had a way of sticking in the public's mind (Errol, Humphrey, Montgomery, Franchot–even then his eye was on the silver screen), he settled on Lambert Hanes.

After the release of *Jalopy Joe*, he catches the first showing at his local theater. Whenever he comes on the screen, it is all he can do not to elbow the strangers on either side of him and point out his fleeting image. His screen credit comes near the end of the reel, after the best boy and the key grip and the gaffer, after the song titles. By the time Lambert Hanes scrolls across the screen the only person left in the audience has to be jostled awake by an usher.

Though it does not come naturally to him, (he's never been that good one-on-one), he speaks to anybody who might be able to help advance his career: producers, agents, actors, directors, assistant directors. They are all nice enough, but he detects in their attitude toward him a certain reserve. He isn't surprised when these contacts fail to bear fruit, and blames it on his own tongue-tied efforts to promote himself. But over time he is confirmed in a growing suspicion: that he is up against an industry-wide prejudice, a stigma that comes with being a double–or rather, a stand-in. (Though once acceptable, "double" is now considered defamatory.) Like all stand-ins, Michael is dismissed out of hand as a talentless non-actor, as an overpaid do-nothing, as a bit of a joke.

He buys a one bedroom apartment in Burbank. It is spare in a Japanesy sort of way: a few pieces of rattan furniture, a boukhara rug, a brass floor lamp, a color TV. He spends little time there over the next few years, a testament to Duncan Avery's enduring popularity. The actor's preference for action roles necessitates location shoots all over the world. Michael explains his long absences to the neighbors by telling them he is a paper salesman. His father, in fact, sold paper products–cups and plates and such to small grocery chains—for some thirty years. He has learned not to tell people the truth. The moment he does, he finds, they start asking you to get an autograph for them or they want you to talk about the great man. "What is he *really* like?" They never want to know about you, only him.

Through a contact with the UCLA film school, he lands a substantial part in a student film about the homeless. It feels good to be acting again. In his first death scene ever, he expires among stray cats and overturned trash cans. There is some talk of wider distribution, of entering the movie in this or that film festival, but that's all it is, talk.

Then, in a whirlwind stretch, he does nine movies, all as Duncan Avery's stand-in. He wangles a screen test with a major studio but they never get back to him. He hires an agent but all she can get him are bit parts with fly-by-night independents. Doing picture after picture, he realizes, is taking away from time better spent pounding the pavement, knocking on doors. He knows he should get out of the stand-in business, but that is not so easy. He's gotten used to a steady income; he's finally beginning to building up his savings; retirement is not so far off.

Increasingly he asks himself the question: What has Duncan Avery got that I don't have? There is that damn smile, of course, but otherwise... We look almost exactly the same: handsome in a vulpine sort of way.

I can act as well as he can, probably better. He has not led a life more virtuous or exemplary. On the contrary, he is a libertine, a rakehell. Then why is his name at the top of the credits and mine at the bottom? Why is he...? He stops just this side of self-pity.

Teeter-Totter is being shot on location in Washington D.C. The story of a returning GI torn between his responsibility to his wife, a paraplegic, and his love for his Vietnamese mistress, it stars Duncan Avery in his first dramatic role since the roundly panned *The Bishop's Daughter* and is considered something of a career risk. Late on this March evening in the nation's capital, the crew, along with some extras and stand-ins, are working within a cordoned off section of the Kalorama area. (The actors slipped away earlier for a reception at the British Embassy.) Standing on the sidewalk behind sagging ribbons of yellow tape, a large crowd has gathered under a street light. Preparation begins for a shot of Michael stepping out of a taxi cab, paying the driver through the window and then turning toward the front door of one of the townhouses.

Climbing into the back seat of the cab parked at the bottom of the hill, he discovers he's forgotten one of his props, a flight bag he left in the stand-in trailer. Feeling overheated in his stiff Air Force uniform, he heads up the middle of the street. He is about a hundred feet from the crowd when someone shouts, "There he is!"

Everyone surges forward, pushing against the yellow restraining tape. Women wave scarves and purses, men stand on tip-toes and yell; others, their arms hanging limply at their sides, simply look on in awe and silence. As Michael draws nearer the excitement grows. Flash bulbs go off. People thrust magazines and bits of paper at him for autographs. A chant goes up: "Dunc! Dunc! Dunc!" Michael has been mistaken for the actor before, of course, but never has he felt its pull so keenly. He knows he should find a way to end this unintentional charade (removing his hat would probably do it), but he can't seem to resist and drifts closer and closer to the sidewalk. Without thinking, he steps into the glow of the street light. Immediately someone says, "It's not him." He watches as the rapturous faces begin to fall, first those in the front and then on back through the crowd. Staring back at him are eyes full of disappointment, disgust, anger. Someone else says, "It's just his double."

He skulks quickly away.

During the filming of *Killer Force*, while Duncan is having an affair with Kim Basinger, Michael woos her stand-in. Afraid of coming on too strong, however, he delays in making the first move and she is snapped up by one of the prop men. He longs for the day when, renown and celebrated, his shyness will cease to be a factor in his personal relations. Sought after from every quarter, he will be spared the difficult and painful work of initiating love affairs and solidifying friendships. Others will happily do these things for him. True, many will want to be his friend because he is Lambert Hanes, movie star. But what was wrong with that? It will be an improvement over his current circumstances, where, since he is timid by nature, the supplies of new intimates are low and always threatening to run out. People of all sorts were eager to know a really successful person.

Michael attends the Hollywood premier of *Teeter-Totter* alone, sitting in the back row. No one knows he's there, which is fitting, since no one knows he's on the screen either–though he is, more than twenty times, seen and yet not perceived, an illusion within an illusion. Midway through the movie he indulges in the fantasy that everyone at this grand affair has come to see him and only him, that they wait impatiently for his split second appearances, and that all the rest of the movie–the dialog, the close-ups, the love scenes–is merely filler.

Duncan Avery, after almost twenty years as a top box-office draw, wins his first Oscar.

Michael walks by all the big shiny trailers, each with a gold star on the door, each, he has heard, with its own fully stocked bar, home entertainment center, fax machine, among other amenities. The sky is cloudless, a cobalt blue. All around him are the mountainous vistas of northern Arizona. He hops a low wooden fence and arrives at the rusting, weather-beaten trailer opposite a row of Port-o-Johns. Stepping inside he finds the other stand-ins crammed into the sparsely furnished cabin. Like himself, they are all dressed in cowboy garb: western shirts and bandannas, boots and chaps, guns and holsters... They sit in old director's chairs and eat from box lunches, paper plates balanced precariously on their knees. The sounds of happy mastication mix with the creak of leather and the jangling of spurs. It is lunch time on the set of *Prairie Dog*, the new blockbuster comedy-western from Metrolux.

Sandy hands him a box lunch and a Fresca.

"I'd like a coke."

"If I'm not mistaken, Michael, you're on a diet."

Among the more degrading aspects of his job is keeping up with the fluctuations in Duncan's weight. Whenever the actor puts on a few pounds, Michael is expected to take food supplements. Whenever Duncan loses weight, which he has recently, Michael is supposed to monitor his caloric intake.

"Just give me the coke, will you."

Shaking his head, Sandy plucks one from the cooler and tosses it to him.

"Mesquite turkey breast," Earl says, holding up the sandwich. "It's very fresh."

"And these pickles," Rick says. "They're so crisp."

Michael looks around at the men in the wobbly chairs, stuffing their faces under ten-gallon hats. They are satisfied with so little, he thinks. Motioning in the direction of the deluxe trailers, he says, "I wonder what they're having. I bet it isn't cold cuts."

Sandy squints hard at him.

"Well, I bet it isn't."

"I heard they had ten pounds of jumbo shrimp flown in," Earl says.

"Jesus Christ. Shrimp."

"For scampi."

"They're having fucking shrimp scampi?"

"Eat your lunch," Sandy says.

As if to spite himself, Michael takes an enormous bite.

"Oh," Rick says. "Congratulations."

"For what?" Michael says, his mouth full.

"What do you mean for what?"

"I didn't win the goddamn academy award. He did."

There is a brief silence. After some token chatter the conversation takes its customary turn. "A neat thing happened with Burt," Earl begins. "I was doing a light check when he came over and asked me about my kids. Right out of the blue. I was so touched. He talked to me for like five minutes."

Approving noises are heard.

Then Michael says, "But Earl, you don't have any kids."

"I know that. But I still appreciated it. It showed he was interested."

"Warren asked about my wife," Rick says. "He always does when it's been a while between pictures. 'What's Maggie up to?' he'll say, or, like today, 'How's Maggie?'"

"Burt shook my hand, too," Earl added, assertively.

"How's Burt's grip, by the way?"

"Very firm."

"Clint's is more of a squeeze than a shake–but it's firm. You feel it."

"Kirk places his left hand on my shoulder when we shake," Tod, the old veteran, says. "Ever noticed that? He just kind of rests it there."

"He does that with everyone," Michael grumbles.

"I've noticed it," Earl says, frowning at Michael.

He can't take it a second longer. "Do you all have any idea how ridiculous you sound?"

"Michael," Sandy says.

"Have you ever listened to yourselves? If just once you could hear–oh, never mind." He throws his lunch in the garbage and stomps out of the trailer, slamming the door behind him.

Sandy catches up with him across from the Port-o-Johns. They smell the apparently subtle fragrance of freshly cut roses, actually the deodorizer wafting over from the portable toilets. "I'm very worried about you, Michael," Sandy says, his small gray eyes crinkling.

"Why? It's all those pathetic losers back there you should be worried about."

"I know what you're going through. I went through it myself. We all do if we stay in this business long enough. For me it was right after *Dirty Harry*. That's when things really took off for Clint. Suddenly I didn't know who I was anymore. My life wasn't real to me. I was angry, confused." Sandy shifts his tall gangling frame, resting a hand on the butt of his pearl-handled revolver. "Aren't you even a little proud of him?"

"They don't care what we think. They don't care anything about us."

"They do, though. They just don't always show it."

"He wasn't that good in *Teeter-Totter*."

"I'll pretend I didn't hear that."

"He wasn't. OK, the part was a bit of a stretch for him. He cried in one scene. He showed some emotion for a change. Big deal." Michael moves away. "If you'll excuse me, I have to get ready for my next big scene. What is it this time? Oh yeah. I get off my horse and tie it to a hitching post. O, Lee Strasberg. Where are you when I need you?"

A black Mercedes careens around the corner of the Boulevard St. Germain. Poking out of the tinted rear window is the barrel of a rifle. Michael and Sandy, who have been sharing a bag of roasted chestnuts on the sidewalk, reach inside their top coats and pull out their handguns. They fire twice at the passing vehicle and then dive for cover behind a pissoir.

"That was a good seven seconds, easy," Sandy says, dusting off his trousers. It is the fifth day of a scheduled ten day shoot. The film, *Buddy System II*, is a sequel to the popular suspense thriller about a pair of rogue FBI agents fighting international terrorism on their own terms.

"They'll cut it," Michael says.

"Not all of it they won't." Sandy invites Michael to join him for lunch at a nearby cafe. "I hear they have a wonderful croque-monsieur."

"Some other time."

"Hello?"
"Is this the Regency Dinner Theater?"
"Yes it is."

Michael is calling from inside a tabac on the Rue St. Jacques. He has plugged his left ear with his index finger in order to hear over the jukebox and video games. "I hope it isn't too late to call," he says. There is a nine hour time difference.

"Is this Mr. Hanes again?"

"Yes, ma'am, it is. I was wondering if you'd posted the cast for *My Fair Lady* yet?"

"I think I told you yesterday, Mr. Hanes. We won't be making our final decision about casting until later this week."

This past Saturday, in Burbank, Michael happened to read in the paper that open auditions were being held that afternoon at a local theater. He drove over at the appointed time. During his reading, Michael wasn't a bit nervous. He didn't flub a single line. His early training in musical comedy came in particularly handy. When asked to do a few bars from "I'm an Ordinary Man," he thought he improved a little on the talk-sing technique Rex Harrison used when he played Henry Higgins by nailing some of the higher notes with his still respectable baritone.

Michael couldn't be more excited about returning to his theatrical roots. He wonders why he didn't think of it before. Unfortunately, the studio called the day after the audition and informed him that the Paris shoot was being pushed ahead two weeks, so that Duncan can put in an appearance at the People's Choice Awards.

"I don't mean to be a nuisance," he says.

"I can tell you this much, Mr. Hanes. We're all very impressed with your resume. *Ambush* happens to be one of my favorite movies. And both of my children just loved *With Extreme Prejudice*. Although to tell you the truth I don't remember you in either film."

"I had small roles in both pictures. My best work ended up on the cutting room floor."

"It's a director's medium, isn't it?"

"It is."

Michael doesn't want anyone to know about his plans, but when Sandy knocks on his hotel door with free passes to the Moulin Rouge, he says, "Sorry, I can't." He waits a beat and adds, "I have to study my lines."

He watches with pleasure as incredulity creeps over Sandy's taut, leathery features. "You have lines?"

"I'm up for a part."

"A part? What movie?"

"It's not a movie." Michael tells him about the audition. Then, for Sandy's benefit, he names all the actors he can think of who went on to stardom after first honing their craft in the legitimate theater: Lawrence Olivier, Peter O'Toole, Richard Burton, Anthony Hopkins...

"Well, uh–you'll certainly be in good company."

That night he reads the script of *My Fair Lady* from cover to cover. In front of the bureau mirror he sings "The Rain in Spain" with gusto and just the right amount of wry pedantry. He has some ideas for the role he can't wait to try out.

In the morning he reports for work at the Eiffel Tower. Because Duncan and Clint's scenes require numerous retakes, he has to wait around for seven hours before the assistant director is ready for him. After riding the elevator to the Tower's topmost deck, he is shot from the ground waving a white handkerchief while leaning over the railing. It is the final seconds of a key scene in the movie, one that marks a crucial turning point in the plot, a distinction he might once have relished.

He goes in search of a telephone and, at the end of a narrow alleyway, puts through the long distance call.

Moments later he hears, "We look forward to your being a member of our cast."

Michael cannot suppress a little victory yelp.

"I'm sure you'll make an excellent Lord Boxington."

"Who? Lord Boxington?"

"That's right."

"I'm sorry, but there must be some mistake. I read for the part of the lead, Henry Higgins."

"Yes, and you did very well. Though not as well as Ron Wilson. Ron played Professor Higgins at Burn Brae last year, and at the Longworth Music Fair the year before that. We feel very fortunate to have snared him."

"But Lord Boxington's nothing but a walk-on part. He only has three or four lines."

"Two. If it's any consolation, and I know it will be, we were so impressed with your audition that we'd like you to be Ron Wilson's understudy. There's no guarantee you'll get to do the role, of course. The important thing is that you'll be working closely with a truly gifted artist."

John Picard

After he hangs up, Sandy, who has followed him, steps out of the shadows. "I'm sorry, Michael."

"Once a double, always a double."

"Don't denigrate yourself that way."

He takes a deep breath and blurts, "Why does he have everything and I have nothing?"

"You know I can't answer that. And it's not true that you have nothing. You have a very good life, in many ways." Sandy puts his arm around Michael's shoulders. He leads him back down the alley and out onto the crowded sidewalk.

"It's not fair," Michael says.

"No. It's not. How about going for an espresso?"

Michael doesn't answer.

Sandy claps him lightly on the back. "We can't all be movie stars," he says.

The next day, the last in Paris, shooting takes place at the Arch of Triumph. Duncan is being filmed in a series of close-ups, the Arch featured prominently in the background. Michael, who's dressed identically to Duncan in a slate gray suit, dark tie, short-brimmed hat and black shoulder holster, paces back and forth in the front of the stand-in trailer. When there's a break in the filming, he walks over to the actor, his right arm extended.

"Michael," Duncan says, taking his hand, visibly surprised at this greeting as they've been working together every day for more than a week.

"How are you today, sir?" Michael says.

"I'm fine. Just fine."

"I wanted to offer you my congratulations."

"Congratulations?"

"For the Oscar."

Duncan Avery smiles his complicated smile. "Thank you. Thank you very much."

"No one deserves it more."

"I appreciate your saying that. Very kind of you."

The actor's personal assistant breaks in and tells Duncan that he is already late for a TV interview.

Duncan has not yet let go of Michael's hand. He gives it a prolonged squeeze before returning it to him. "If you'll excuse me," he says.

"Of course."

The assistant director shows Michael where to stand. He removes his coat and drapes it over his shoulder. He pushes his hat slightly forward, partially obscuring his face, as he's been instructed to do.

"Roll'em."

Michael begins his slow walk through the Arch, his head bent low. He can still feel in his palm and fingers the pressure of Duncan's firm grip. It's as though the actor had put something extra into his handshake, something that he wished only Michael to know.

Tics

My father promised me five dollars if I stopped jerking my head. "Is it a deal?" he said.

"Yes, sir."

"And here." He handed me two quarters. I'd already received my allowance for that week. The fifty cents was an advance, a vote of confidence, and I pocketed it guiltily. I knew it was hopeless.

"Just try," Mother pleaded. She was sitting on the bed. She glanced over at Father, who had turned back to the paper work on his desk, then looked at me. "That's all we ask. OK?"

"OK."

She frowned, dubious.

I asked to be excused. I couldn't wait to get away. I'd remained perfectly still under close scrutiny for almost ten minutes, and I didn't think I could hold out much longer. I was dying to twitch, fidget, squirm, but most of all move my head in that way Father found so disturbing he was willing to confront me about it personally. Usually he dealt with me through Mother.

She said to him, "Is there anything else you wanted to say?"

Father lit a cigarette, then shuffled the papers on his desk. I guessed he was as embarrassed as I was.

As I turned to leave, Mother asked what I had in my hand. While trying not to move in any obvious way I'd kept my hand balled into a tight fist. "Nothing," I said.

She shook her head at me. She knew my tricks. "Go," she said.

I waited until I got to my room to pry open my hand, one frozen finger at a time.

That week I spent as little time as possible in my father's company. I ate and ran, I played outside. If I watched TV I sat towards the back of the living room, where I was free to indulge in surreptitious nodding and twitching. I was bearing a new burden. It wasn't the money, which, of course, was unattainable. It was the new awareness that Father had his eye on me. He wasn't a demonstrative or expressive man, and before our talk I could always tell myself he didn't really notice or wasn't much bothered by my head-jerking, and all the other nervous mannerisms that had preceded it. Realizing he'd been observing me all along, I felt terrible, especially since there was almost nothing I could do about it.

I felt even worse knowing that Father blamed himself for my condition. Mother had confided this to me as soon as I was old enough to understand. It was a familiar story by now. One rainy night when she was five-months pregnant with me, Father had tried to pass a tractor trailer on a two-lane highway and collided with a pick-up truck. The driver of the pick-up was drunk and had neglected to turn his lights on. Mother was thrown from the car and ended up spending a month in the hospital. For the first week the life of the unborn child was in jeopardy. When I was born Mother and Father were assured by the obstetrician that I had emerged a perfectly normal baby. But as an infant I cried continuously. And later on, I was unable to sit without rocking in place. I could not be still. They became concerned, the doctor's assurances notwithstanding, that I had suffered some sort of prenatal injury, a jolt to the nervous system, perhaps, or a subtle deformation of the spine. They had hoped the wound, as it were, would heal itself, or that I would somehow outgrow it. But by the time I started school I seemed, if anything, to be getting worse. I began to shift from one nervous habit to the next. I was only nine when the dentist told my parents that from incessantly grinding my teeth I'd worn all the enamel off my bicuspids, and that if I didn't stop soon there'd be nothing left of them. After that, I switched to cracking my wrist, repeatedly rotating my hand in such a way that it produced a loud popping noise. This one Mother found particularly irritating.

There followed two or three others, and then, finally, my head-jerking. Actually, it was more like a sharp nod than a jerk. Done too often, the jerking motion–tilting the head back, holding it there a moment, then bringing it down quickly, ending with an emphatic snap–would give me severe head and neck aches. Each time I went through this ritual, each time I fell into any of my nervous antics, I hoped it would be the last, that my body's craving for movement, as punishing and as violent as I could make it, would be satiated. The collision with the pick-up truck was not my father's fault in any real way, but to all of us at the time it did seem like the best explanation for my weird compulsions.

On Sunday morning Mother entered my room as I was getting ready for church. She closed the door behind her. Father, who worked nights and slept late, didn't go to church, for which I was grateful. Trying to remain still throughout the long, Sunday worship service–to the extent, at least, of not drawing attention to myself–was a weekly torture.

Mother was silent. Finally she said, lowering her voice, "Yesterday your father was watching you through the kitchen window. He saw you out in the backyard, doing that with your head. He broke down. He cried, Joey."

I was stunned. I'd never known my father to cry. "I'm trying," I said. "I really am."

"Your father loves you very much," Mother continued. "Even though he doesn't always show it, he cares, very deeply. And naturally this upsets him. It's not your fault, of course, but it does upset one. You used to drive me crazy with your cracking."

"I can't help it!"

"I know that. We both do. We understand, but..."

"But what?" Frustrated, I was close to tears myself.

She stepped towards me. She wore a pearl-grey suit and matching pumps. She'd had her hair done the day before, a permanent that always added an inch or two to her height. "Bow your head, Joey." She began to pray, asking God to deliver me from my affliction, to drive out from my body this thing that was causing such pain and worry.

I'd ceased to believe a lot of what I'd been taught about religion, though not so much I didn't wonder if I wasn't at least partly responsible for my tics—if not their origin, then their persistence.

"Mama?"

"Yes?"

"Was Daddy really crying? You know, crying crying."

She nodded gravely. "Like a baby."

For some time after that, every night before I went to bed, Mother would join me in my room and we would pray for a miraculous cure. I began to show signs of improvement, though not for the reason my mother imagined, and not enough to lay claim to the five dollars. I'd entered a transitional period. I was in the process of eliminating my head-jerking the only way I knew how, by replacing it with something else, something I hoped would be less glaring to my parents, and the world. (For the first time, I'd begun to draw curious stares from the schoolmates.) It consisted of a simple flexing of the stomach muscles, creating a barely audible expulsion of air, a snuffle. For a while, I had it under control. But as with all my little habits, this one soon got out of hand.

In the middle of one of my mother's prayers, she stopped abruptly. "What was that?"

"What?" I said.

She continued to pray, then stopped again. I opened my eyes. Her face was contorted with reproach and disbelief. "What are doing *now*?"

"Nothing."

"Don't tell me that. I heard you. What was that noise? It sounded like...it sounded like some wild animal."

I couldn't help myself.

"That!" she exclaimed, and jammed the fingers of one hand into her permanent, raked her hair until she stood with her head in the crook of her arm. "Oh, Joey," she said. "What are we going to do with you?"

There were no more prayers.

Despite good-faith efforts to stop or redirect it, my new compulsion escalated into a variety of louder and more disagreeable noises. I would sometimes wake up in the morning with sore stomach muscles and a scratchy throat from the previous day's exertions. Before long I had so alarmed my parents with my honking and grunting that they decided it was time they took the step which, Mother confessed to me, they'd been putting off for years. The moment had arrived to seek professional help. "Your father's willing to pay whatever it costs. He's very generous that way. Maybe now you'll appreciate him."

I was taken first to our family physician. One morning Mother drove me to his office. I knew it well, for I was always coming down with colds and flus and missing entire weeks of school at a time. But I'd never had a physical before. The doctor began by asking me questions about my health and general well-being. It was then it came out that I'd been having trouble sleeping.

"You never told me that," Mother said, and laughed. She shook her head at the doctor as if to say, He's at that secretive age.

Mother left the room and the doctor put me through a series of tests, all of which I'd had before, though never in a single appointment, then he asked her to stop back in.

I was fine, he said, except that my blood pressure was rather high, a possible sign of nervous stress. He turned to me. Besides insomnia, was I aware of any other symptoms?

"He fidgets," Mother broke in, "among other things. He's done it his whole life, since he was a baby. You may have noticed it yourself."

The doctor asked me if I was under any sort of emotional strain.

"I don't think so."

Was something bothering me, something at school, on the playground, at home?

I thought about it, but nothing came to mind. "No."

"Doctor," Mother said. "There's something you should know."

She proceeded to describe the accident, weaving into her narrative the theory of pre-natal injury.

The doctor nodded when she was done. He couldn't dismiss it out of hand, he said. He had heard of such cases, but there wasn't much that he, an ordinary GP, could do. If she desired, however, he could write out a prescription for a mild sedative, something to help quiet my nerves.

Mother put her hands together. "Please," she said.

It was decided that I needed to see a specialist. His office was in the next county, more than an hour away. I was apprehensive. I must be pretty bad off, I thought, if my parents were willing to go to all this trouble. I was curious, too. As many times as it had been explained to me I could never quite grasp what it was a chiropractor did.

In the depressing little waiting room–plastic chairs, months-old magazines, salmon-colored walls–Mother stammered, "They...well...they adjust things."

"What kind of things?"

"I don't know. Bones and things." She said to Father, slumped over a ragged issue of *Newsweek*, the brim of his favorite hat, a brown fedora, shielding his face, "Milton. What is it they do?"

"Does it hurt?" I asked.

"Joey," Mother said.

"What?"

"You know what?"

I'd been honking.

Father glanced up at Mother. "Did he take his pill?"

"Did you?"

"Yes," I lied. I was supposed to take my sedative twice a day, but I usually skipped the one in the morning. It left me feeling tired and groggy and did nothing, as far as I could tell, to relax me.

"Does it hurt, Daddy?"

It was rare I asked him a direct question, but I felt I had the right. I was the one going in there to have my bones adjusted.

He looked up at me, eyes narrowed under the brim of the fedora. He reached inside his coat for his cigarettes, lit one, then laid the match on the lip of the ashtray. He was as smooth and controlled, as graceful really, as I was edgy and high-strung. I was his son, yet we were so different, which made it easy to believe that early on I'd had my nerves shattered, perhaps irreparably. I'd tried many times, as often as I could stand to think about it, but I was unable to imagine my father in tears.

He dragged deeply, his hands cupped the length of the cigarette, like a movie star tough-guy. He expelled the smoke through his nose. He said, "You do whatever this man tells you." Then he went back to his magazine.

Mother almost lurched from her chair. "Jo-ey!"

The following Monday we went to a local clinic to have my brain waves checked. I did my best to keep still as the nurse attached the metal wires. One end of the wires was connected to a machine with a lot of dials and a panel that looked like a huge graph. The other end the nurse covered with bits of putty and stuck to various places on my head. I felt like a character in a horror film, bound to a chair by the mad scientist, my personality about to be radically altered with the flip of a switch.

When the nurse had finished with her preparations she went and stood in front of the machine.

"What's happening?" I asked.

"Nothing," Mother said. "Nothing yet." Father wasn't there. He'd chosen to wait in the car. I was confused by this, his apparent indifference, but I figured out later that it was a simple matter of not wanting to see his only child with wires sprouting from every part of his head. Mother added, "It'll all be over in a minute."

"What's wrong with them, my brain waves?"

"Be still."

I then asked the question that had been preying on me for some time. "I'm not crazy, am I?"

"Hush."

"Am I?"

"Don't be silly. Of course not."

"So what's wrong with me then?"

"That's what we're here to find out, isn't it?" The nurse looked over. Mother beamed at her. "It's his first time," she said, absurdly. The nurse went back to her dials.

"Will it hurt?"

"No."

"That's what you said about the chiropad...the chiropod..."

"Forget *him*."

The chiropractor, I knew, was a sore subject. He'd done no more than run around cracking the bones in my neck and back, and at one point drove his knee so forcefully into my spinal column that I cried out, more in surprise than agony, it's true, but the memory was still one of great pain. Neither was I any better for the experience. I wasn't a bit less nervous. Father paid the man but he'd nixed the idea of more appointments, which the doctor insisted were necessary for a complete recovery.

The nurse was ready, and I braced myself as the machine began to whir. I felt nothing, to my great relief, and the test was soon over. The wires were removed, the putty picked from my hair, and I was asked to step from the room while the nurse conferred with my mother.

In the car on the ride home, Mother and Father whispered in the front seat. The suspense was awful. Mother had been very somber, uncharacteristically taciturn, as we walked from the hospital to the parking lot, and now I was frightened. I might be crazy after all.

"What did they say?" I asked.

Neither of them spoke.

"How did I do?"

Again, no answer.

"How am I?"

Mother twisted around in her seat. She looked tired, fed up. She said, heavy with disappointment, "Normal."

Father read about Dr. Ishee in the newspaper. The neurologist had made a name for himself by treating patients with symptoms similar to my own:

uncontrollable twitching, violent tics, involuntary jerking of the limbs. I wasn't as bad as that, of course, but–my parents' thinking went–so much the better. I was that much closer to being cured. His fee, Mother pointed out to me, was seventy-five dollars, for one fifty minute session. If Father was prepared to pay out that kind of money, she said, the least I could do was cooperate. As if I might object. In the six months since I'd had my brain waves checked, my condition had worsened. Now, rather than confining myself to a single habit, I was moving freely from one to the other, grinding my teeth one moment, popping my wrist the next, and so on. At night I would lie awake for hours. During the day I could never unwind sufficiently to nap. My school work suffered accordingly. More upsetting to me than poor grades, however, were my classmates who now delighted in teasing me. My futile attempts to remain still while sitting at my desk had turned me into an object of fun, sometimes ridicule. I was as eager as my parents to resume the search for a successful treatment, whatever the cost.

A distinguished gentleman in a dark suit and red tie, Dr. Ishee greeted us in the foyer of his large, beautiful home, located in one of the best neighborhoods. Before shaking Dr. Ishee's hand, I noticed, Father removed his fedora, and the doctor accepted Mother's hand with such delicacy I thought for an instant he would bow and kiss it. They were both awed, even intimidated, by the man's wealth and bearing, and I shared with them the hope that they had brought me, at last, to the right place.

The neurologist directed Mother and Father to a small waiting room at the end of the hall. I exchanged a last look with Mother, a silent affirmation of what she had told me on the drive over: "Make sure and tell the doctor about the accident, first thing. Don't forget."

I sat across from Dr. Ishee in a plush, black leather chair. Without any prompting I launched into a short, breathless account of that tragic night over ten years ago now. Then I ran through a brief history of my symptoms. The doctor listened carefully as I spoke, nodding and making notes on a white pad. But when I was done he made no comment. Instead, he asked me to stand up, then to extend my arms and touch my nose. After that, he had me walk a straight line, putting one foot directly in front of the other while looking at a fixed point on the wall. Returning to my chair, I thought dismally of the chiropractor.

Dr. Ishee sat down and put his pad aside. He observed me a moment, then he said, "You don't seem that nervous to me, Joey."

"I don't?"

"No."

"I'm kind of controlling it right now."

"Most of my patients can't do that. Consider yourself lucky." He added, "Neurologically speaking, there's nothing wrong with you. Your balance is good, your hand-to-eye coordination normal. How do you feel?"

"OK."

"I mean in general, most of the time."

"Pretty bad, like I said." I was losing patience. He seemed to have forgotten everything I'd told him before. The story about the accident hadn't made the slightest impression. He acted as if he knew better, as if I were keeping something from him. "I've been having trouble sleeping."

"Yes. You mentioned that."

Dr. Ishee leaned forward, his hands folded between his knees. "How are things at home, Joey?"

"Fine."

"You have a good relationship with your parents, do you?"

"Yes sir."

"Describe it."

"Describe it?"

"Yes. If you don't mind."

Mother had a strict rule against discussing them with other people, but I thought I might make an exception this one time. It could be part of the treatment, for all I knew, and I wanted Father to get his money's worth.

I'd been talking for a good half hour when the neurologist stood up and went to get my parents. He asked me if I'd mind sitting in the waiting room by myself for a few minutes. I passed Mother coming in. She looked from me to Dr. Ishee with a sweet and knowing smile, as if she'd been eavesdropping on us and found everything to her liking, as she knew she would.

In the waiting room I picked up a magazine and made myself comfortable. Direct sunlight was coming through the low, casement windows. I felt tired suddenly and arranged myself on the couch, stretching out so as to catch a maximum of the warming rays. I let the magazine fall from my hand and closed my eyes.

In what felt like the next minute, Mother was standing in the doorway. "Come on," she said, and waved her arm at me.

"What is it?"

"I said come on."

I followed her out into the foyer. Dr. Ishee was walking straight for us, his hands upraised in a gesture of entreaty or helplessness. Father was nowhere in sight.

Mother pushed me past the doctor towards the front door.

Outside, I saw that Father was already in the car. I heard footsteps behind me. Dr. Ishee was hurrying down the walk with Father's fedora.

Mother opened the back door for me, slammed it shut, then jumped in front. She hollered over the seat, "What did you say to that man?"

"Huh?"

"What did you say to the doctor? What did you tell him?"

"Nothing. Nothing much."

"Don't lie to me." She paused. "Milton, your hat. You left your hat."

As if he hadn't heard, Father put the car in gear and began backing up. Just then Dr. Ishee appeared outside my window. He pointed at the hat, then made a cranking motion. As I was rolling down the glass Father applied the brakes, then quickly accelerated. Arms limp at his sides, the fedora hanging from the fingertips of one hand, the doctor watched us go.

Mother seemed confused and distracted by all the commotion. But by the time we reached the first intersection she'd gathered her wits. She looked over the seat at me. "All right. The truth," she demanded.

The truth was, I didn't recall saying anything to make her so upset. I'd gone on about her and Father in a general way, I thought, their relationship with each other, with me. I was careful not to reveal anything too personal. I hadn't wanted to say something that could be used against me later on. So much for that.

"I don't know," I began. "I told him about you and Daddy and how–"

Mother cut me off. "And how horrible we were, right? How we'd been mistreating you all these years."

She couldn't have said anything to me more shocking. "No," I protested.

"How it was all fault," she continued. "That we were to blame for your...the way you are."

"I didn't say that, any of it. I swear to God."

"You what?"

I was forbidden ever to swear, or take the Lord's name in vain. "Sorry."

"Don't ever let me hear you say that again? You understand me?"

"OK. I told him—"

"Do you?"

"I said I was sorry. I told him him about the accident, like you said. I did. He wasn't interested."

"The fool," Mother said, for her unusually strong language. "You can't trust these doctors, not a one of them," she said, more to Father than to me. We were on the main highway now, picking up speed. "Pay them a lot of money and they think they can say anything. Any lie." She looked back at me again. "I don't mind for myself, but to sit there, all high and mighty, and criticize your father, your father who has done everything he could think of to help you, who has spared no expense... What else did you tell him? There must be more to it than that."

"That's enough," Father said.

"You must have said something to—"

"That's enough," Father repeated, louder this time. "Leave him be."

Mother stared hard at him, her eyes running over his face and up to his bare head. Father always wore a hat when he drove the car, or was otherwise in public. It was strange seeing him behind the wheel without it. Bald on top, what hair he had left formed a ring of wavy fringe. Mother continued to stare and finally drew from Father a sharp glance. They looked at each other a moment, then faced the road ahead.

No one spoke the rest of the way home. As soon as Father pulled into the driveway, Mother jumped out and went inside the house.

Father sat with his hands on the wheel, gazing out towards the garage.

"Want me to open it?" I said to break the silence, referring to the garage door.

"No," he said, and punched the car's cigarette lighter.

We remained like that for a minute or so, not speaking, the car filling up with cigarette smoke, the only noise an irregular ticking sound, the motor cooling. I didn't want to go in alone and have Mother start yelling at me again. But I felt a wave of nervousness coming on–I had already given my head a few jerks, after making sure Father wasn't watching in the rearview mirror–and decided I'd take my chances in the house. I opened the door.

"Wait," Father said.

He put out his cigarette, then pulled from his wallet a five-dollar bill. He held it out to me. "Here."

I shook my head.

"Go on. Take it."

"No"

"It's yours."

"I don't want it!" I'd done nothing to deserve the money, and I didn't understand, did not want to understand, why it was so important to him that I accept it.

I pushed my door the rest of the way open. Just then I felt a sharp tug on my shoulder. Father had reached over the seat and was now pulling me back into the car. With a wildness that both amazed and frightened me, he seized me by the wrist, then clutched at my hand. He pressed into my palm the five-dollar bill. As if he still feared my resistance, he closed my fingers over the money, hard, until it hurt.

John Picard

Inga

L ane walked from his office to the mail chute opposite the bank of elevators and dropped in the white envelope. There had been instances of letters getting stuck in the chute and he listened as it fluttered down. Smiling, he turned and pressed the down button. He was pulling on his gloves when Fletcher from Accounting came around the corner and they boarded the elevator together. After the doors closed, Fletcher asked Lane if he'd care to go out for a drink. Ordinarily he would have refused. He hardly knew Fletcher, and he didn't like to drink and drive. But today he had something to celebrate. "I would, yes, very much."

"I know this great place right down the street."

They stepped into the lobby just as the postman was entering the building. Lane glanced back in time to see him emptying the mailbox, scooping into his sack hundreds of envelopes, his among them. "That'll be just fine," Lane said.

He followed Fletcher out of the building and down the sidewalk, assuming they were headed for one of the posh watering holes along K Street. But he had just opened his umbrella–a penetrating drizzle was falling–when Fletcher threw out his arm, hailing a cab.

A few minutes later they were passing into a somewhat questionable part of town, lots of boarded-up buildings and suspicious types hanging out on street corners. Lane hadn't recognized the address Fletcher gave the cabbie and hoped he wasn't taking him to some dive. Lane preferred bars that were on the fancy side, clean and nicely decorated, the kind with complementary peanuts and a lock on the bathroom door.

He began searching his mind for conversational openers, but quickly realized he and Fletcher had nothing to say to each other. A big man with curly graying hair and glasses that looked too small for his large head, Fletcher had only been with the company since the end of the year. Lane ran into him sometimes at the coffee machine, and once they'd found themselves at the same lunch counter and chatted a while about inconsequential matters; but that was it. Lane was about to comment on the weather when Fletcher, despite the No Smoking sign, lit a cigarette. He took a long drag, then cracked the window, holding the burning ash close to the opening.

"How've you been getting along over there without Inga?" he said.

Lane was unable to suppress a smile, for more than anything else just then, it was his administrative assistant he most wanted to talk about. It was to Inga that his white envelope, now safely on its way to the post office, had been addressed. She had called in sick all that week (she'd sounded wretched on the phone), her longest unscheduled absence since she started in Governmental Affairs. Lane had missed her more than he ever thought possible, missed seeing her at her PC, elbows pressed to her sides, fingers moving lightly over the keys, missed the frank, open smiles they exchanged from their desks at least once every day. They had been working virtually side by side for three years now, and he'd always cared for Inga, but until this week he hadn't known how much. Tuesday he'd locked his office door and typed a letter into his PC and printed it out; not a love letter, nothing mushy, merely a declaration of his special feelings for her. What made him bold was that for a long time now he'd suspected that Inga, who, as far as he knew, was unattached, had a little thing for him too. It was not uncommon, after all, secretaries falling for their bosses. He had put the letter in an envelope with her name on it and placed it in her in-box. But the next day she hadn't come in and he'd passed another restless night, wondering if tomorrow she would return and discover his letter. But she was quite ill apparently and had failed to come to work yet again. She might be out all week at this rate. And so, late that afternoon, he had written in her address under her name, posted the letter...

"We're managing," Lane said. "Although we miss her, of course. The whole department does."

"A damn fine worker, it seems to me," Fletcher said.

"We don't know what we'd do without her."

"What's her typing speed? About how many words a minute?"

"Eighty, eighty-five."

"That's what I hear."

Lane noted that Fletcher's pants' cuffs rode halfway up his calves, revealing thick, white, hairy legs. Lane wore extra-long socks with elastic at the tops to avoid just this problem.

Fletcher put his hand out the window, let the wind take his cigarette and rolled up the glass.

Lane said, "We feel very fortunate to have someone of Inga's caliber and experience."

Fletcher nodded. "She thinks very highly of you, too."

Lane was a little surprised to learn he'd been discussed by the two of them, but Fletcher tended to roam the whole office, bending everyone's ear.

The cab stopped in front of a squat one-story building. A kelly green neon sign flashed the name of the bar and a tiny shamrock. Little Irish bar, Lane thought. The worst kind.

Mall Kane's had a low water-stained ceiling and a sticky wood floor and reeked of beer and disinfectant. There was a long row of stools covered with cracked green leather. The bartender sat at the far end perched under a TV watching the news. The dozen or so customers were mostly seedy types, unshaven, bleary-eyed men in shabby clothing.

"National Premium's only a buck here," Fletcher said, climbing up on one of the stools.

"Great."

Lane considered his options. A Scotch straight up would be best; that much less liquid in his system. A brand Scotch, Chivas Regal, would be ideal, as a reward for his decisiveness today. But Fletcher was talking beer, and since he'd been kind enough to invite him along, Lane thought he might as well get the same. One wouldn't hurt.

Fletcher waved the bartender over. After they'd ordered, he said to Lane, "This is some joint, eh? None of that blond wood and ferns crap."

"I know what you mean."

Fletcher drank his beer in one gulp. A little breathless, he set the mug on the bar and wiped his lips on the back of his hand. Lane too was thirsty and before he knew it had finished most of his own beer. Fletcher, meanwhile, had fallen into some sort of funk. Slumped over the bar, he was peering gloomily into his empty beer mug. "God, oh God," he said.

Lane asked him if he was all right.

Fletcher didn't seem to hear. Slowly rousing himself, he lit a cigarette, blew three floppy smoke rings and watched them break up over the tiered rows of liquor bottles. "How long you been with the company, Lane?"

"Six years."

"Six years. You must like it."

"I do. Very much." Actually, he found being the oldest paralegal in the department embarrassing, more so every year. He was older now than many of the attorneys. He'd tried dressing younger: bright knits ties and colored shirts. He'd even let his hair grow over his ears, but it had only made him look silly. Pushing forty, he was still trim, no fat on him, but he looked scrawny more than anything, prematurely worn. He'd thought men were supposed to improve with age. It was as painful to look in the mirror sometimes as it was to see at the bottom of his desk drawer his pile of law catalogs. He had one from each of the area law schools but had never gotten around to applying.

Fletcher was shaking his head. "Do you know this is my fourth job in five years? And I was lucky to get that, considering my employment history. A year here, a year there. Terrible." He looked at Lane. "I envy the hell out of you, I really do. Me, I'm too damn restless." He set his glasses on the bar and rubbed his eyes. "It's like a sickness." Then he hollered at the bartender to bring him a pitcher of beer. Lane had been thinking about switching to Scotch, but it was too late now. He supposed he could get away with a second glass of beer.

"You married?" Fletcher asked.

"No, I'm not."

"That's smart. That's intelligent. I can't say I'm surprised, though. First time I saw you I said, Here's a fellow with something on the ball. I could see right away the kind of person you were. You take care of yourself. You're in control. Inga says you're the perfect boss."

"Well, she's the perfect administration assistant."

The beer was getting to him after all, together with all the coffee he'd drunk that afternoon. Without Inga he'd had to answer his own phone and type his own memos. Whenever things got busy he always drank more coffee than usual. He recalled having his last cup around four. Assuming, of course, that he would be heading straight home, he hadn't bothered to use the office toilet; a nice one: two stalls with functional locks.

Fletcher was digging in his back pocket. He brought out a black leather wallet and handed it to Lane. "Open it."

Inside the wallet was a fold-out stack of photographs.

"The family," Fletcher said.

They were mostly pictures of two little girls, one with dark curls, the other with bangs that covered her eyebrows. Both had wide faces and big front teeth. The rest of the pictures were of a handsome woman with high, sharp cheekbones and a serious expression.

Lane gave back the wallet. "They're very attractive."

"They're fuckin' beautiful." Fletcher lit another cigarette. His hands shook. "Margaret's amazing. Margaret's my wife. She's forty-one and she just got her Ph.D."

"Impressive."

"Medieval literature. I didn't even know there was such a thing and she gets a degree in it. I'm damned proud of her."

"You should be."

"Puts her mind to something and does it. She's an admirable person in many ways. Cold, though. Frosty woman. Know what I mean?"

Lane nodded uncertainly.

Then Fletcher suggested they have shots of Bushmills. Noting there was still most of a pitcher to get through, Lane mentioned that he had to drive home.

Fletcher chuckled, "Don't we all," as if it were a purely philosophical matter.

"And I'm short of cash," Lane added.

"Don't worry. It's on me."

The drinks came.

"Mud in your eye," Fletcher said and downed his whiskey in a single gulp. Lane sipped his.

Fletcher swiveled on his stool, bumping Lane's knees. "I guess you play the field."

"What?"

"You see lots of different women, I suppose."

"Oh yes."

"What kind do you like? What kind of women?"

"Oh, I don't know. All kinds."

Fletcher reached over and patted his shoulder. "My man."

The truth was he'd practically stopped going out. He'd had a few dates right after his wife left him (she'd complained he was too staid for her, too undemonstrative; Mr. Stiff, she used to call him), but that was almost five years ago. He'd finally stopped missing her, but he was often lonely, especially on weekends. Every day he came home from work and fixed his dinner, then tended his plants, then a little TV, a mystery novel and to be bed, always the same. It wasn't enough, he knew that now, a realization that had as much to do with his decision to make his feelings known to Inga as anything. He thought of her now. Tall and slender, she had clear, pale skin, wore her blond hair piled on top of her head and, slightly pigeon-toed, walked with an endearing shuffle. He knew she was no beauty, but he liked the way she looked. Sometimes he would glance up and find her standing in his doorway, poised to ask him a question but too polite to interrupt. Lane placed his shot glass on the bar. There was no denying it; he was definitely needing to use the bathroom. Fletcher was staring into his beer mug again, a good time to check out the facilities. He excused himself.

As he feared, the bathroom door would not lock; the doorknob hung loosely from its socket. Inside, he found a urinal and an exposed toilet, but no stall. There were maybe twenty men in the bar, all of them heavy drinkers (the only kind Matt Kane's attracted), and any one of them might choose this moment to relieve himself. He positioned himself before the urinal, his eye fixed on the door. He forced out a spurt, then another. He'd just gotten something going when he heard footsteps outside the door. No one came in, but then he heard more footsteps, and that was that–he was completely plugged.

When he returned to the bar, Fletcher was refilling their mugs. He proposed a toast. "To friendship," he said.

Lane brought his mug to his lips, and, allowing the beer to slosh against them, pretended to sip. He noticed Fletcher eyeing him and worried that he'd been found out. Fletcher continued to stare. "Listen," he said at last, "I don't want to bullshit you. I know I couldn't if I wanted to. We're not best buddies or anything. I'm aware of that. But I have to talk to someone and I've always respected you. You're not into gossip like the rest of the office. I think you can keep a secret. Am I right?"

"Yes, of course."

"I'm in bad way, Lane." Fletcher held out his hand. The thick, stubby fingers trembled. "I have no one else to turn to." Fletcher paused, then he said, "I've been seeing Inga. Over two months now. Does that surprise you? If it does, it's OK. In fact, I'd prefer that."

Lane said nothing.

"Did you suspect? Were you on to us?" Fletcher waited for him to answer.

"No."

"Good. If you didn't notice, maybe no one else did. It makes me feel a lot better your saying that."

Lane picked up his shot glass and took a big sip. The whiskey burned all the way down. He wasn't used to swallowing so much at one time and almost gasped.

"You see," Fletcher continued, "Margaret knows. She senses things and she figured it out. So she gave me a choice, you know. And I told her I'd end it. And I did. That's why Inga hasn't been at work. She's all broken up. When I told her I couldn't see her again, I meant it. But lately I don't know. Lately I've been weakening."

To soothe his throat Lane drank some of his beer. When he saw what he was doing he moved his mug and his shot glass to the edge of the bar, so he wouldn't be tempted again. It didn't really matter, though. His bladder had already begun to ache.

"She's like no woman I've ever known," Fletcher went on. He made his hand into a fist. "The passion of this woman, the sheer animal vitality. My God, man, the things we did, the mountains we climbed. What do you think of Inga?"

Lane forced out the words, "She's very nice."

"You know what I mean. As a woman."

This he refused to say.

"Very reserved, right? Very quiet, but...hot. That's the beauty of it. No one would ever guess that about Inga. I know didn't. I thought, Who is this creature, this wild thing?" Fletcher leaned closer. "She used to make this noise, Lane."

"I'm not sure that's any of my business."

"Kind of a chuffing sound. *Chuff, chuff, chuff, chuff—*"

"I'm going to have to be running along soon," Lane said. "I'm expected somewhere."

"We'll just finish this pitcher. The thing is, I don't think I can give her up." Fletcher stared hard at Lane. "I bet you think that's crazy, a man like you."

"As I said, it's none of my business."

Fletcher blinked, and raising his mug, proceeded to take tiny tips from it, as if to prolong the evening.

Lane would have insisted on leaving if he hadn't decided to try the toilet again. "I'll be right back," he told Fletcher.

In his rush to get to the bathroom, he came in on someone standing at the urinal, a grizzled character in a baseball cap and a soiled sweatshirt. The man didn't seem at all bothered by the intrusion but Lane, retreating, apologized anyway. Lane had been trying not to think about it, but while he waited parts of his letter to Inga began coming back to him. The lines that before had seemed to him rather formal, almost businesslike, now struck him as horribly personal and revealing. One line caused him particular embarrassment: "I don't think it presumptuous to say that you don't find me entirely unappealing." How was it that he was still capable of such delusions? What would she think of him now? The man came out. As Lane was walking in, Fletcher appeared at his shoulder and they entered the bathroom together.

At the urinal Lane unzipped his fly and struck the attitude of someone calmly relieving himself. Fletcher had lifted the toilet seat. He stood with his feet wide apart and promptly produced a stream of liquid as thick as a rope. It thundered in the bowl.

"Want to hear something amazing?" Fletcher said. "I've never seen my wife naked. She won't allow it. Isn't that incredible, in this day and age?"

Lane zipped up and flushed. His kidneys were pulsing with pain. Feeling panicky, he went to the basin and washed his hands. There were no towels and he wiped his hands on his pants' leg.

Fletcher, who hadn't bothered to wash, opened the door for him. "After you."

At the bar Lane remained standing next to his stool, to show he meant business. "I think I mentioned I have to be somewhere."

Fletcher frowned at the unfinished pitcher. "One more for the road."

"I'm late as it is."

"Hey. No problem." Fletcher drained his mug, took out his wallet and plopped down a ten. "My treat."

Normally he would have fought for the check, but not today. There wasn't a moment to spare.

They stepped outside. It was dark now and the rain had picked up. Miraculously, a cab was coming down the street right then and pulled to the curb. Lane's hopes rose a little. He might just make it. He pictured his bathroom at home, the pink and black tile, the matching towels hanging beside the sink, the generous commode.

"I didn't mean to chew your ear off back there," Fletcher said in the cab. "It's just that I'm at a crossroads, you know. And I could really use some advice." He looked at Lane for a long moment, as if he hoped some might be forthcoming. "Let me put it another way. What would you do in my situation? A wife who won't walk bare-assed in front of you—then there's Inga."

Were they really discussing the same person: the shy, shuffling woman he'd worked with all these years? What did Inga see in this crude, pushy, beefy— this married man?

Fletcher laid his hand on Lane's shoulder. "Put yourself in my shoes."

Lane looked at the hand, but Fletcher didn't seem

John Picard

to notice. Then he asked pointedly, "What about your children?"

"I know. God, I know. But I think they'll understand, once they're older, once I explain it to them. And they know what Margaret's like. I mean, she's their mother, right?"

They stopped outside the company parking lot. Fletcher insisted on covering the cab fare as well. Lane got out and headed down into the garage. He would have gone on up to the office toilet, but on Fridays they locked the building for security reasons at six sharp. He could hear Fletcher's rapid thudding footsteps behind him and took out his keys, ready for a quick getaway. He'd gotten the car unlocked and was pulling the door open when Fletcher came up and stood in front of him. "Isn't there any advice you could give me?"

"You have to decide for yourself."

"So you think I should drop her."

"I really don't care."

"Tell you what. I'll leave it to you. I'll do whatever you say."

"Do it," Lane said.

"Do what?"

Wincing, Lane got in behind the wheel and closed the door. Sitting was difficult; it helped a little to lean to one side.

"Do what?" Fletcher shouted, his face at the window.

Lane started the engine and backed up.

Fletcher was walking toward the car, his arms outstretched. "Do what? *Do what?*"

Lane sped for the exit.

It was a fifty, fifty-five minute drive to his apartment in the Maryland suburbs, depending on the traffic, which could have been better. People were out celebrating the end of the work week. The rain made everything worse. Turning up Connecticut Avenue, he went by several restaurants and hotels, quality places certain to have excellent facilities. But parking was a problem: there were no spots anywhere. If only he could hold out a little while longer. Unfortunately, he seemed to be catching all the red lights, and whenever he passed someone he ended up behind a car waiting to make a left turn. To make up for lost time, he occasionally exceeded the speed limit. Not by much. He didn't want to be pulled over; that would be death.

He crossed the District line; nothing but suburbs from here on out. He accelerated to forty, passing brightly lit neighborhoods and teeming shopping centers. He might have considered pulling over and running into the woods if there'd been any. He thought of Fletcher making his way home, when and where he would next relieve himself the last thing on his mind. He wondered if everything Fletcher told him was true. It seemed incredible. But what did he know about such things? No woman had ever chuffed for him.

Lane pressed the brake pedal. He had inadvertently climbed up to sixty. Then, all at once, he knew it was hopeless. He was more than twenty minutes from home, a tremendous amount of time given his present state. His back was killing him and it felt like his bladder had expanded, crushing his other organs.

He kept an eye out for any dark areas between the houses, places out of the glare of street lights. He was passing through one of the better neighborhoods, big two-story homes with white pillars and spacious lawns. He turned off the highway onto a side street, went down a couple of blocks and pulled to the curb. He was surprised to hear his own breathing. He was panting. He eased himself out of the car. The wind blew rain into his eyes and mouth. Unable to stand properly, he was forced to take short steps. Hunched, he started down the sidewalk.

He came to what appeared a suitable spot, a substantial patch of darkness between two large homes. There were lights on in front, but nothing on the side. He walked onto the grass, crouched low. He heard a dog bark. He wasn't sure of the direction. The pain seemed to have affected his senses. He took a few more steps before he saw it; only the dog's immense white spots were visible. Snarling, it came at a gallop, throwing itself against the wire fence which until then he hadn't seen. Barking maniacally, it leapt again and again at the fence. Lane backed away and felt his leg snag on something sharp. He heard the fabric tear as he disengaged his trousers from what must have been a rosebush. He hurried back to the sidewalk. His leg was throbbing. His hair and face were drenched. His shoes, good Italian leather, were probably ruined. A car rounded the corner. Lane straightened himself a little and tried to lengthen his stride. He thought: Mr. Stiff.

He came to a big split-level at the end of the block. Its lawn covered half an acre. Its only light was a tiny amber porch light. He went around to the side, alert to dogs and rosebushes. He opened his fly. He was so backed up that at first it only came out in spurts, then in a slow steady stream. It was a relief without being truly pleasurable.

He was zipping up when a window in front of him suddenly filled with light. Its glow spread over the lawn to a cement birdbath not far from where Lane was standing. The window's curtains were drawn and he could see into what looked like a dining room. A middle-aged man in a purple robe entered the room and sat at a long table. He opened a magazine and flipped the pages. A woman wearing shorts and a T-shirt came in. She handed something to the man and sat across from him. The man and woman opened their mouths wide and for a moment appeared to be singing to each other. Then it looked like they were trying to swallow their fists. It was a minute before Lane figured out they were flossing their teeth. Shivering, he watched until they were done. He stayed there until the couple got up from the table and turned out the light, and even a little while after.

Nixon: The Man And His Muse

"**A**nd, Diane, I want you to find out everything you can about Emily Dickinson," the President said.

This direct order came at the end of a meeting with his press staff, dealing with the recent break-in at the Democratic National Headquarters in the Watergate Complex and the arrest of five men rumored to have ties to CREEP, Nixon's reelection committee. I found it an odd request to say the least, and normally I would have asked for an immediate clarification, but Nixon was out of sorts that morning, groggy from lack of sleep, with a full slate of legislative business ahead of him. I knew from experience that at such times he was impatient with questions that impeded the flow of his brilliant, if overburdened, mind.

"Yes, sir," I said.

"This is nothing but a third-rate burglary, but the Democrats will try to use it against us. They're already trying. Well, if they think Nixon's going to just sit around and take it, they've got another thing coming. We'll hit back, and hit back hard."

Dismissing us with a wave, he took up a yellow legal pad and swiveled in his chair until his back was to the room.

Outside the Oval Office, I asked Ron Ziegler, my boss and White House Press Secretary, "Why would the President want information about a nineteenth century American poet?" The President's antipathy to the arts has been greatly exaggerated, though it's true he tended to associate them with his liberal enemies and the Eastern elite, a prejudice, as will be seen, not sufficient to extinguish a dormant enthusiasm and a profound appreciation.

"I have no idea. Can you believe how he was shouting at me in there? Why doesn't he like me? I do everything he asks. My support is unwavering."

"He likes you. He thinks of you as a son practically. Well, a son-in-law."

"I don't mind being his whipping boy, but I wish I got credit for it once in a while. What were we talking about?"

"Nothing, Ron. Back to work."

While researching in the Library of Congress, I had plenty of time to ponder why I'd been chosen for this strange assignment. I was a recent graduate of Wellesley and been labeled, quite undeservedly, the "brainy" one on the staff. I'd studied Dickinson in two of my college literature courses, and been a devotee of her poetry since childhood. But the President couldn't have known that. It might also have to do, I thought, with Nixon's traditional view of the sexes, women being more inclined to literary matters than men, especially men like John Erlichman and Bob Haldeman, his closest aides, "the Nazi's," as Dr. Kissinger referred to them. But none of this explained the motive behind the President's request.

That came three days later when I presented him with sixty double-spaced pages that included poems, a brief biography, some criticism, all bound together in a beige, loose-leaf notebook.

"It's not everything," I told him. "She wrote almost two thousand poems, and there's a wealth of scholarship that I didn't even—"

"Who's this?" the President said. He was pointing at the only known photograph of the poet, aged only sixteen, which I had photocopied and pasted on the cover.

"Emily Dickinson."

"What's it for?"

"You said you wanted everything I could find about Emily Dickinson."

"Angie Dickinson. Kennedy's old mistress. Not Emily Dickinson." All but forgotten now, in her day Angie Dickinson was one of Hollywood's reigning starlets.

We looked at each other, then burst out laughing. Contrary to the popular perception, Nixon enjoyed a good laugh as much as anyone else.

"Oh, Mr. President. I feel so foolish."

"This better not leak, Diane," he quipped. "We can't let my enemies think I'm getting soft."

We tried and failed to determine whether he'd misspoken or I'd misheard; not that it mattered. It was Nixon's habit to blow off steam by giving orders he never expected his staff to follow up on, his directive to Haldeman during a rough patch in the Paris Peace talks to nuke Hanoi being a good example. He'd already gotten over his momentary pique regarding the break-in, having been assured by his aides that it was of minor consequence, and would be of no use to the Democrats in the upcoming election.

I was only 26 but, looking back, I think my youth and inexperience were among my chief assets. It was 1972, the year Nixon opened up relations with China and created detente with the Soviet Union, the year of the Christmas bombing that expedited the end of the Vietnam war. That was the greatest year of a great man's presidency, and I was smack in the middle of it. Certainly, being chosen America's Junior Miss when I was seventeen (my more beautiful sister, Linda Sawyer, had been first-runner up the year before) and winning the $5000 scholarship that led to four idyllic years at Wellesley was a huge thrill, as well as affording me valuable life experience. But nothing could have prepared me for jumping directly from my one misguided year of law school into the White House, my only protection from paralyzing fear being my naivete, along with a belief in the man whose goals for America I was fortunate to advance in some small way.

In addition to my duties on the press staff, I occasionally served as an "anecdotalist," one of numerous staff members assigned to accompany the President throughout his work day and record examples of his warm, human side–Nixon the Man, as it were–and then leak them to friendly media outlets. It was an attempt by the White House to show an aspect of the President that a hostile press either refused to see or ignored.

I was present when he thoroughly charmed the Ambassador of Nepal with stories of his superior skill at poker and other games of chance. I overheard his comforting words to a congressional aide whose wife had just died of cancer: "There, there now." During a ceremony in the Rose Garden, I saw him twice touch the forearm of that year's poster child for the United Way. But I wasn't the one who first noted evidence of the President's new passion.

"The Old Man said the strangest thing when he was briefing Goldwater on the Mideast," Ron said. "'I dream in possibility.' Isn't that weird?"

"Not at all. I think it's very apt." I recognized the line, of course, and then remembered that at my meeting with the President I'd accidentally left the Dickinson notebook behind. "He does dwell in possibility. Are you going to release it?"

"No way. Too fruity."

With growing concern, Ron came to me a few days later with a quote gleaned during a visit by Jordan's King Hussein. He closed the office door and recited, "'We never know how high we are till we are called to rise.' What the hell's that supposed to mean?"

"It's a line from Dickinson."

"Kennedy's girlfriend?"

"Emily. The poet."

"Jesus Christ. If it gets out the Old Man's quoting poetry to world leaders, the press'll kill him. Talk to him about it, will you? He'll listen to you."

"Don't be so alarmist. The President deserves to have a little beauty in his life."

"Not until after the election, he doesn't."

Naturally, I said nothing. I'm not sure if Ron did, though something he said the next day triggered a Presidential scolding I could hear on the other side of the door to the Oval office. I was still there when Ron came out, head bowed and face flushed, followed by the President who, looking invigorated, gave me a sly look. "'Anger as soon as fed is dead.'"

"Mr. President, I think you've been reading your Emily Dickinson."

"Thanks to you, Diane. Great gal," he said, though whether he was referring to me or the Belle of Amherst, I couldn't say.

"Presentiment is that long shadow on the lawn," Emily wrote, and indeed the gloom that descended on the President in the days after his landslide reelection, his joyless victory, suggested he had some inkling of the agonies to come.

After the Watergate hearings convened, highlighted by John Dean's assertion of a "cancer on the White House," the President was seldom in Washington, opting to stay at Camp David, Key Biscayne, or Fort Lauderdale, all the while discussing Watergate strategy with his aides. When he wasn't huddled with his advisors, he reserved large blocks of time when he was alone with only his thoughts and his yellow legal pads.

Then came the revelation of the White House taping system, and the tug of war between the courts and the administration over the release of the tapes. Nixon's isolation increased. He drank too much. He indulged in obsessive viewings of the movie *Patton*. The staff feared for his sanity. How much more could the Old Man take?

"She was like me," he said when I was with him in Key Biscayne. "She preferred paper to people. Once she didn't leave her house for five years. She didn't see anyone. That sounds like heaven to me."

"Amherst's only ninety miles away from Wellesley, but I never made it to The Homestead. I've always regretted that."

"The Homestead?"

"Her house. The Dickinson mansion."

"She had the right idea. I'd shut myself up in a room and never come out too if I could get away with it. I wouldn't have to deal with the press, the back stabbers in my own party, that damn Judge Sirica. I'd read and write and to hell with everyone else." He made an abrupt, sweeping gesture with his arm.

"She had her family, sir. She lived with her sister and her mother. She wasn't totally cut off from–"

"I wish I'd had a sister, instead of those dead-beat brothers of mine. My mother...my mother was a saint. So was Emily's."

He also observed,

"They say Nixon's a liar. I'm not a liar. 'Tell all the truth but tell it slant...The truth must dazzle gradually/ or every man be blind.' People can't take too much truth, Diane. I've always known that. I've lived by that. I only give them a little at a time. I speak the truth, but indirectly–slant."

Later in that awful year, when he was holed up in his office in the Executive Office Building, listening to tapes of his Oval office conversations from which his enemies hoped to find criminal evidence, he was reminiscing, as he often did then, about the high points of his administration.

"The protesters called me the mad bomber. I wasn't mad. I was perfectly sane. I have feelings. I didn't enjoy being responsible for the deaths of little children in Hanoi. How did she put it? 'For I have but the art to kill–without the power to die.' There were times when I wanted to chuck the whole thing. What is it the kids say? Drop out. But that would have been the easy way. I had a job to do. I had to stop the war, I had to bring the peace."

I said I didn't recognize the poem he'd quoted from.

"It begins, 'My life had stood a smoking gun.'"

"Are you sure about "smoking gun," sir? Isn't that what your enemies are looking for?"

He scowled. "I might have that wrong," he said. In the past we would have shared a laugh over this; now he slipped the headphones back on and hit the play button.

Both the House Judiciary Committee and the Special Prosecutor subpoenaed White House tapes in their investigation of the President. Rather than turn them over, he released edited transcripts. I read all 1,254 pages of them. My faith in the President was unshaken. I knew that Nixon, a complex man, had his dark side, and that Haldeman and Erlichman brought it out in him like no one else. The transcripts showed someone who could be crude, hate-filled, even bigoted. What they did not show was the dynamic world leader, the visionary statesman, and the sensitive reader of our greatest poet.

I wanted to express my support to him personally and asked Ron to speak to General Haig, the new chief of staff, about allowing me some private time with the President.

Ron said before I went in, "He called me twenty-two times yesterday, half of them after midnight. He's worried about his legacy. He's afraid the only thing he'll be remembered for is Watergate. Don't say anything about the hearings or that traitor, Dean. He's supposed to phone Golda Meir at noon and I don't want him upset. And something else. You know about the Old Man's leg, right?"

The President had recently been diagnosed with phlebitis. He was only days away from the start of a seven nation tour of the Mideast. If the blood clot lodged in the vein of his leg broke lose and entered his heart or lungs, it could be fatal.

"If you get a chance, see if you can talk him out of it? God knows I haven't had any luck."

The bags under the President's eyes were mousy gray, his jowls had taken on a perceptible wattle, his hair was mused. Always meticulous about his dress, he was clad in a rumpled sweater and a pair of khakis. It was sad to see this man of action, who prided himself on eating the same lunch every day in five minutes (salad and cottage cheese) and never having time to exercise, sitting at his desk, doing nothing.

"Mr. President, I wanted to tell you how much I respect you, and everything you've done for this country. I hate what they're doing to you. I think you should fight them, Mr. President. I think you should fight them all the way."

"I've never been a quitter."

"No, sir. And there's no reason to start now."

"I didn't do anything wrong."

"I know that."

"Everything Nixon's done has been for the good of the country."

"And the country thanks him—you—for that."

He stared at me for a long moment and the mood changed. "You're a lovely girl, Diane." It was the first time ever he'd complimented me on my appearance.

"Thank you, sir."

"You must have had your pick at Wellesley."

"I beg your pardon."

"Boys. I'm sure they were standing in line."

"Well..."

"I couldn't get a date when I was in college. No one would go out with me. I was poor. I didn't have the fancy clothes and the new car. I wasn't part of the in crowd."

"Didn't you meet Mrs. Nixon in college?"

"I had to beg her to go out with me. If I wanted to see her, I had to drive her and her date to the malt shop or whatever. It was embarrassing, but I did it. She came from a respectable family, you know. They didn't think I was good enough for her. Nobody did."

"You certainly showed them, Mr. President."

"No matter." He stood up and walked to the window overlooking the south lawn, heavily favoring his left leg.

I commented on his limp, expressing my sympathy.

"The doctors say I should stay off my feet. They say I could die if I make this trip."

"It does sound risky. Wouldn't it be better if you–"

"'Afraid? Of whom am I afraid?/ Not death: for who is he?' She was tough, Diane. Tough as nails. She only published ten poems in her lifetime, you know, and even those were edited without her permission. They took out all the dashes. They changed her syntax. You can't do that without changing the whole meaning! They tried to destroy all her hard work. But she didn't let that discourage her; she never stopped writing. I draw strength from that."

"But regarding your health, sir. With all due respect: 'Because I could not stop for Death,/ He kindly stopped for me.'"

"No matter," he said, and fell silent. Shoulders hunched, hands clasped behind his back, he stared out over the Ellipse, the Washington monument gleaming in the distance.

I did not make the trip to the Mideast, but, watching him on television, I winced as he limped along beside Sadat or charged into the ecstatic crowds in Cairo, heedless of his personal safety.

"He wants to teach them a lesson," Ron said the day of the President's return. "He wants to go out a martyr." In only five days Nixon would leave on yet another trip, this time to the Soviet Union, the site of one of his greatest foreign policy triumphs. "When I try to talk sense to him, he just stares at me. He doesn't even yell anymore. I can't take it, Diane. I can't take what they're doing to him. You know what I wish sometimes?"

"I think I do." More and more of the staff had been leaning toward Nixon's resigning.

"I know he did some dumb things, like letting Colson hire that psycho, Liddy. But he doesn't deserve this humiliation. If he doesn't resign, they'll impeach him. And the Senate will probably convict. The whole world's against him. His back is to the wall. I really wonder what keeps him going sometimes."

Any hopes that he would save his Presidency with a demonstration of his popularity abroad were dashed when the Supreme Court voted unanimously that he had to turn over all the tapes requested by the Special Prosecutor. He spent that weekend at Camp David with his family and his advisors, reviewing more and more tapes, discussing his next move.

Monday, August 5. Arguably the worst day of my young life. I, and the rest of the staff, read the transcript of the President's conversation with Haldeman about using the CIA to block the FBI's investigation of the Watergate break-in, a clear case of obstruction of justice. I couldn't believe it. I was devastated. For two years Nixon had lied to his family (poor Julie, tirelessly pleading her father's case before the public), his friends, his lawyers, his aides, and to the American people, about his role in the cover up. He didn't tell it slant; he didn't tell it at all.

The entire White House seemed to be in tears. No work got done. Staffers sat at their desks in silence, or fetched a bottle and drank.

"When this gets out, Ron, he's finished."

"I need to talk to you about that. If he resigns, and he still hasn't said for sure, he wants you to join him in San Clemente as part of his post-Administration team. He wants people around him he can trust."

"Trust is a two way street. I'm not interested."

"I understand how you feel. But you're young, you'll get over it."

"Don't patronize me. You're not much older than I am, and I won't get over it."

"This is no time for grandstanding. Your President needs you. Now more than ever."

"He's not my President."

"Diane!"

I was angry, I was hurt. "Pain has an element of blank;/ It cannot recollect when it began..." Not always, Emily.

The next day I was still smarting and insisted, as only a headstrong, disillusioned twenty-seven year old can, that Ron relay to the President at once my decision to pass on San Clemente.

I was waiting for him when he returned from the Oval Office. "What did he say?"

"Nothing."

"He must have said something, Ron. He must have had some reaction."

"He looked crushed, but that's how he always looks now. You and the President...there was never anything...you know?"

"I won't dignify that with a response."

"It's just that you two always had this bond."

"Well, it wasn't that."

"Whatever it was, I expected a little more loyalty from you."

"He lied to me."

"He lied to me, too. What makes you so special? He lied to the Secretary General of the Soviet Union. He lied to everybody. He lied to himself."

"I don't think I'm special."

"Yeah, you do. Wellesley this, Wellesley that. America's Junior Miss goes to Washington. In case you didn't know, the whole staff thinks you're a snob."

"In case you didn't know, the whole staff thinks you're an ass."

There was a lot of squabbling and venting of this sort. But with the release of the June 23rd transcript, "the killer tape," as it was known around the White House, frayed nerves were replaced by a portentous calm. The call for his resignation was nearly universal. Leaders of his own party were banging on the door, urging him to step down. Yet he held on, as if savoring the last important decision of his Presidency.

There was no question of skipping work that Wednesday. The media were going crazy trying to find out what was happening inside the White House, and it was all we could do to keep them at bay. But I didn't want to be there. I hadn't slept. I couldn't seem to go more than thirty minutes without tearing up. I was physically exhausted, emotionally muddled. When I received a call from General Haig telling me to be at the White House heliport at fourteen hundred hours, I was surprised on the one hand, since, having rejected his job offer, I doubted I'd ever be in close proximity to the President again; I was agitated on the other hand, assuming we were in for a whirl-wind trip to Camp David, another futile attempt by Nixon to outrun fate.

"Not a word of this to anyone," General Haig said as he escorted me to the helicopter. "Ever." He looked at his watch. "You should be back by seventeen hundred hours. Christ almighty, I can't believe I agreed to this."

"Agreed to what, General?"

He stepped away, the pilot secured the door, and seconds later we were in the air.

Besides myself, the only passengers in that part of the helicopter were two secret service agents and Manolo, Nixon's manservant. Minutes later we landed at Andrews, the home of Air Force One. This would not be a quick hop to the Maryland foothills.

"Does anyone know where we're going?"

Either they had been sworn to secrecy, or didn't know themselves. There was a short delay while the President boarded the plane, then it was our turn and we were airborne again. Twenty minutes into the flight I was summoned to the President's quarters. He was sitting next to a window, looking out with his chin in his hand. With a listless wave, he indicated the seat across from him. He was shaved, his hair was combed, he was neatly dressed in dark slacks, a white shirt and jacket, but his recent weight loss made him look gaunt and haggard. He would not, or could not, look me in the eye.

"Recognize that down there?"

"I don't believe I do, sir."

He said we were flying over Massachusetts.

"I hope you don't mind me asking, Mr. President, but where are we going exactly?"

He broke into a weary grin. "To the source, Diane."

"The source?"

"The Homestead."

I was being given a gift (and an apology, I realized later), and from the moment he revealed our destination until we landed at Westover Regional Airport, where we piled into the waiting bullet-proof limousine and started the high-speed drive to Amherst, I felt all the shock and gratitude of a young girl winning a beauty contest. At the same time, I knew this trip was for him as much as it was for me, that after what he'd been through, and what he now faced, he needed it, needed it desperately.

The modest motorcade–the limo plus two secret service vehicles–cruised down North Pleasant, then made a left on Main Street, blocked off at either end. We passed Evergreens, her brother's house, then pulled up in front of The Homestead.

We peered through the tinted windows at the two-story, brick structure, the surrounding fence, the four white columns.

"In her wildest dreams," I said, "she couldn't have imagined that a President of the United States would–"

"'Wild Nights, Wild Nights, were I with thee...' Let's not keep her waiting any longer, Diane."

As we were walking up the steps, flanked by secret service agents, I noticed that his limp was negligible. I found out later his phlebitis had improved, but my impression at the time was that, Lourdes-like, he had set foot on holy ground and been instantly cured. We entered the mansion and stood in the hall that ran to the back of the house, the stairway to the bedrooms ahead of us and to the right. The Nixon slump was not in evidence. His shoulders were squared, his arms straight down at his sides. His gaze was clear and focused, as if he'd just awoke from a refreshing sleep. Our guide, a middle-age woman stunned and a little tongue-tied at finding herself with such an illustrious charge on what must have been short notice, led us through the rooms on the ground floor, pausing in the kitchen where Emily baked her bread and cakes. As she ran through her spiel, Nixon rocked back and forth on his heels, a sign of impatience. At last we headed up the stairway to the second floor. The guide tried to direct us to the library, the next stop on her itinerary, but the President refused to budge.

"Is this her room?" he asked, jabbing a thumb over his shoulder.

"Yes, sir."

"We'll skip the rest."

"Of course, Mr. President. If I'd known you—"

"No matter," he said, and flashed a lightning grin to smooth over the slight awkwardness.

We stepped to the threshold of Emily Dickinson's bedroom. By now the guide understood that she was the one on a tour and remained silent as the President stood at rigid attention inside the doorway, situated at one corner of the medium size room. From this vantage, her night table and single bed were to the immediate left, her Franklin stove against the opposite wall, her writing desk in the far corner.

After a minute, the President quoted, "'A prison gets to be a home'."

Was this his astute acknowledgement of the poet's insight into her peculiar "lifestyle?" Or was he thinking of the White House? Or was he thinking–this was pre-pardon, of course, but the Judiciary committee had just passed its third article of impeachment and some of his closest aides were already in jail–about the possibility of time spent in a literal prison? Doubtless all three, his mind, like hers, working continually on multiple levels.

We followed him into the room. Standing behind her writing desk, he placed his hands delicately, reverently, on the back of her chair, as one might on the shoulders of a dear friend. I found out later that none of the furniture was original, and I've always been thankful to the guide for not mentioning this. There were samples of the poet's handwriting on the desk.

He took out his glasses. "I don't even think Rose could decipher this scrawl," he said, referring to Mrs. Woods, his personal secretary. "It's worse than mine." He ran his hand over the words, as if absorbing through his fingertips that precious script.

I stood beside the tour guide as the President circumambulated the room. He paused in front of each of the portraits of her family and friends that hung on the otherwise bare walls. He examined the stove, peeked in the closet. He studied her only surviving white dress, now worn by a seamstress's dummy.

When he arrived back at the writing desk, he thanked the guide for her kind assistance. Standing tall again, he surveyed the room one last time. "Now I'm ready," he said.

From the second we left the bedroom until we reached the limo, it was all I could do to hold my tongue. As soon as we were inside the car, I turned to him and blurted, "Mr. President, I've been such a fool. I'd be honored to accompany you to San Clemente. I hope you'll forgive me for being so selfish. Lately, I've been very..." I lost it. The tears came.

"There, there now," he said.

"I've been very confused."

"That's all right. You're not the only one."

"I'd be happy to work for you as long as you need me, in whatever capacity."

He looked directly at me for the first time that day. "Thank you, Diane. I appreciate that. Use this."

I took his handkerchief and wiped my eyes.

So pregnant with feeling was the moment that we didn't speak again until we were back on Air Force One. Soon after take-off, he said,

"Maybe you could do something for me right now."

"Anything, Mr. President."

He reached into his jacket and, taking out a paperback book, handed it to me. It was a selection of Dickinson's poems. "I don't have my glasses," he explained.

In all the excitement he'd forgotten that he'd just used them. "Of course, Mr. President. Is there any one you want to hear in particular?"

He laid his head back and closed his eyes. The plane had just pierced the clouds; sunshine was filling the cabin. "Your choice, Diane."

I would be standing only ten feet away from him when he announced his resignation on live TV the next night. I would go with him to San Clemente and spend four months helping him through that horrible adjustment period. I would be inexpressibly flattered when he asked me to assist him in writing his memoirs, a rewarding labor that lasted two years. Of all the hours I spent in his company, though, the ones I treasure most were those on Air Force One when, thousands of miles above the earth, it was just me, the President, and Emily.

Nimbus

Clara and I were there to have our first look at the new baby. Nan brought Scotty down as soon as he woke up. It was Bob's turn to feed him, but all his efforts were met with screams and flying fists. He finally handed him back to Nan who sat down and lifted her sweater.

"You can't re-refrigerate it once it's been used," she said.

Bob stared dejectedly at the rubber bottle in his hand.

"From now on, why not dispose of it after a feeding."

"Right," Bob agreed.

Nan nursed the baby. I could see the upper part of her breast, including some of the nipple.

"I can't believe you made this," Clara said. She was examining the underside of Nan's dulcimer.

"Actually," Nan said, adjusting Scotty in her lap, "I didn't make the fret board and one or two other pieces."

"Still."

Nan had taken up the dulcimer because music was good for babies.

"Bob? I think Ted could use another drink."

I would have asked for a whiskey, but Clara was always accusing me of embarrassing her in front of "our only friends." Right before Scotty was born Nan had shown us a sonogram of her womb. It was dark and grainy. All you could make out was the shape of a head. I'd had a lot to drink that night. Clara would never forgive me for saying it reminded me of the Shroud of Turin.

Bob took my cup and saucer.

Scotty swung out from Nan's breast and gazed around goggle-eyed. He bore a strong resemblance to his father, large round head, elfin ears, sandy hair. Attracted by Clara's wave, his grin widened ecstatically and he gave a sudden lurch.

"Ouch," Nan said, and pried loose Scotty's grip. "Manhandling your own mother. Shame on you." Laughing, she pressed him gently to her shoulder, slipping a hand underneath to lower her sweater. The baby began playing with her hair, recently cut and styled in the manner of Cleopatra. A hat had left a crease all around the top of her head.

At the first pause in the flow of chatter, Clara said, "We just saw *Notorious*." We had seen *Notorious* some time ago, but it was something to talk about. Bob and Nan had met during their college film class, and movies were important to them.

"Like it?" Bob said, who was bringing in the coffee. He sat cross-legged on the floor.

"Loved it. But I wanted to ask you. In the last scene, where Gary Grant and Ingrid Bergman and... what's his name?"

"Claude Rains."

"Yeah. They're coming down the staircase, right? From what you've told us, Hitchcock never does anything without a reason. Well, is the staircase some sort of symbol?"

Bob turned Nan. "Did Dr. Barr have anything to say about staircases?"

Nan scrunched up her face.

"Sometimes a staircase is just a staircase," I said.

"Not for Hitchcock," Bob chuckled. "We don't have that luxury. In his early films, it's true, he hadn't quite worked out all his symbols, his icons, but by *Notorious*..." He stroked his bushy mustache. "A staircase, huh? It must have something to do with descent."

Nan reached down and patted Bob on the head. "Hitchcock can't put anything over on you, boy." She burst out laughing.

Bob snapped his fingers. "You mean...you mean it's not descent?"

We all laughed. Scotty extended an arm and waved. Catching it by the wrist, Nan kissed his fingertips one at a time.

"Like into hell?" Clara said.

"The lower depths," Bob said. "The abyss. Whatever you want to call it. Have you seen *Vertigo*? You have to see *Vertigo*."

Nan shivered. "It's..."

"Right," Bob said. "The staircase sequence alone is worth the price of admission. I'm surprised Dr. Barr didn't tie that in with *Strangers on a Train*, even *Rear Window*."

"Technically it wasn't a staircase," Nan said. "In *Vertigo*."

"Yes it was. Not that it matters. Thematically, it's the same thing."

"I suppose," Nan said. She took Bob's hand.

"You know what's really fascinating," Bob said. His eyes shifted as he gathered his thoughts. "This just occurred to me. When Hitchcock's inconography matured, when he finally got all this stuff down, the staircases, the train tunnels, whatever, I wonder if he didn't feel like, hey, it's over. I'm done. Because what he's doing is fundamentally self-limiting."

"You mean," Clara said, "he made the same movie over and over."

"No, but he came up against the same barriers, barriers he himself had created."

Clara nodded slowly.

John Picard

"I think what Bob means," Nan said, "is kind of the opposite of what Ted was getting at. For Hitchcock a staircase is never just a staircase."

"It's a staircase," Bob said. "It's just that it's the same staircase."

"Whether he likes it or not," Nan added. She passed Scotty down to Bob and left the room.

As if pondering all this, Clara leaned back in her chair, tilting her head to one side and clasping her hands around one knee. She began to gnaw the inside of her lower lip, another sign that her nervous stomach was acting up. At dinner she'd served herself extra helpings of creamed broccoli and chicken tarragon to show Bob and Nan how much she appreciated their invitation. "That is fascinating," she said.

Bob was playing dive-bomber with Scotty, holding him overhead, then nuzzling and kissing him on the way down.

"He loves that," Clara said.

Nan came back carrying a tray of short-stemmed glasses and a bottle of Armagnac. I asked her if she had any brandy.

"Armagnac is brandy," Clara said.

"No problem," Nan said, retreating with a smile.

To encourage himself to take advantage of his subscription to *Scientific American*, Bob had left several back issues beside his reading chair. I picked one up and turned to an astrochemical study of globular clusters. But before I could scan the first paragraph, Clara had closed the magazine on my hand. Nan, returning with a bottle of Hennessy, pretended not to see.

"The other day," I began, but immediately forgot what I was going to say. I was that bored. It occurred to me that it was the baby's fault, that as it stood, our bond with Bob and Nan was so flimsy it couldn't support the slightest change, let alone a new baby.

Nan asked if anyone would like more coffee.

"I would," Bob said.

"Aren't you afraid you won't be able to sleep?" Clara said.

"It's funny, but coffee has the opposite effect on me."

"That's so weird."

"You weirdo," Nan said, cracking up.

"The other day," I said, "I saw *Raging Bull*."

"Ted went to that one alone," Clara said. "I refused."

"Is that the one about the boxer?" Nan said.

"Jake LaMotta."

"I guess we don't go in for boxing movies. We didn't even see *Rocky*."

I said she didn't miss much.

"You liked it at the time," Clara said. "Remember when we came out of the theater? We were both trembling. You liked it then."

"Well, I resent it now. I resent being set up like that. I can't think of that movie without feeling duped."

"Tell them how you were after *Raging Bull*."

"Stunned," I said.

"Depressed. Depressed is more like it. You drank–he drank four Scotches after he got home."

"The last scene," I said. "'I coulda been a contender.' You've seen *On the Waterfront*."

Bob and Nan, the film buffs, had never seen *On the Waterfront*.

I was hoping to put a little life into the evening, maybe even save it. "In the last scene of *Raging Bull*," I said, standing up, "you've got Jake LaMotta doing his impression of Brando. So it's DeNiro doing LaMotta doing Brando. Talk about icons." I borrowed Bob's fountain pen. "He does the whole scene with a cigar," I explained.

I tried to ignore Scotty's whimpering, but I hadn't done more than a few lines before it turned into a sustained whine.

"He's cranky," Nan said.

Bob bounced the now sobbing infant on his knee. "You little scene stealer, you."

I sat down. Clara put a consoling hand on my shoulder. "It was really good, honey."

Nan wanted to know if I did any other impressions.

"Later," Clara said.

"Anyone else for coffee?" Nan said. "Help yourself to more brandy, Ted." She left.

Bob insisted on pouring my drink despite his problems with Scotty. Taking my glass, he set it on the coffee table and filled it to the lip.

"Whoa," Clara said.

Suddenly Bob got all excited. "See that," he said, nearly dunking his finger in my drink.

"What?" Clara said, moving in.

"See how the liquid rises just above the rim of the glass. It's convex—ever so slightly."

"It is. It really is."

"That's a nimbus."

"A nimbus. I've never heard it called that before."

I had never heard it called anything. "Isn't a nimbus like a halo?" As though merely curious, I asked Bob if he had dictionary handy. Holding tight to Scotty, he fetched one from the den.

"A luminous vapor or cloud or atmosphere," I read, "about the head of a god or goddess when on earth." To be fair, I read the rest of the definitions, none of them touching on convex liquids.

"Must be a new usage," Clara said.

"I don't think so," Bob said. "I've used it my whole life."

"I like nimbus. I think we should call things by any name we want. I really do."

Bob rose with difficulty. "You folks will have to excuse us." He hummed a lullaby as he carried the baby up the stairs.

John Picard

When I looked at Clara she was bent forward with her arms over her stomach.

"You better get to a bathroom," I said. The color had drained from her face and her forehead glistened with perspiration.

While Clara was gone, Nan came in and stood in front of the stairs, listening to Scotty. She smiled as if she were reassured, then walked over and sat across from me in the wicker chair, setting Bob's coffee cup on the table.

"I used to play the zither," I said. "In elementary school."

She fluttered her lashes. I pointed at the dulcimer on the floor.

"Oh," she said. "Oh yes."

"But it didn't stick. I loved the sound, but holding the bow like that always my hand cramp up."

"You don't play the zither with a bow."

"You don't? Maybe it was some other instrument."

Nearing the breaking point, I reached over and began to gulp the coffee.

"I'm sorry," Nan said, "I didn't know you wanted more coffee."

I put the cup down and followed her into the kitchen. On one wall, pots and pans hung from a ceiling-high peg board. The dinner dishes had been scraped and stacked on the counter. I placed them in the sink and turned on the hot water.

"Don't you dare," Nan said. She was pouring coffee into an earthenware mug. "I mean it."

"I don't mind."

"I know but–the Brillo pad's under the sink." She threw back her head and laughed. Removing the wash cloth from the handle of the refrigerator, she took a dripping plate out of my hand, dried it thoroughly and set it on the second self of the cupboard. As I scoured a heavy skillet, she twirled the dish cloth as if it were pizza dough.

"He's quite a guy," I said. "Scotty."

"We think so."

"You weren't disappointed or anything."

"Disappointed?"

"You were pulling for a girl, weren't you?"

"Oh no. We had feeling it might be a girl–which shows what that's worth–but we didn't actually have a preference."

She watched me rinse the skillet, twirling away.

"I like what you've done with your hair."

"Why thank you, Ted."

"You're not letting yourself go, like a lot of mothers."

I had always been attracted to Nan, probably because, Clara aside, she was the only woman I saw on a regular basis socially. I'd had my fantasies, of course, but without thinking seriously of acting on them. Until now, that is.

When handing Nan the skillet, I brushed up against her.

"You smell like baby powder," I said.

"I know," she sighed, as if that were terrible, and went to the peg board, hanging the skillet next to a wok. When she came back I made her wait rather long for a saucer. Then, just as she was taking it from me, I kissed her on the lips. She didn't blink. She placed the saucer on the first shelf of the cupboard, toward the back, then folded the dish cloth and hung it on the refrigerator.

"I think I better check on Scotty. Leave the silverware. And the glasses. We don't want to spoil Bob."

I went back to the living room and looked at the pictures of globular clusters, millions of compacted stars taking up a tiny patch of black space. A disturbing and lonely thought. There were a few isolated points of light at the borders of the photographs, and I concentrated on those, but they ended up giving me the same bleak feeling.

Clara returned and sat on the edge of the couch, hands on her knees, back arched.

"Are you all right?"

She nodded and took a deep breath.

I poured another brandy. "Listen to him, will you."

Scotty was wailing.

"It's not going very well, is it?" Clara said.

"Hey." I waited for her to look up. "You're not responsible for everything that happens. You're so egocentric sometimes."

"I'm sorry I did that with the magazine."

"Forget it."

"I wish we could just leave."

"Where did Bob put our coats?"

"Ted. Please sit down. Ted."

"All right."

I couldn't stop wondering if they had an extension in the bedroom. Did husbands call the police nowadays when someone got fresh with their wives? I finished my brandy.

"I feel much better," Clara said.

"Good."

"We'll have to have them over for dinner, you know. What about two weeks?"

"Four."

"OK, three. Too bad we can't all go to a movie–the way we used to."

"Couldn't they get a sitter?"

"Scotty's a newborn. Newborns don't have sitters. Do you think they can hear us?"

The baby had stopped crying. There wasn't a sound anywhere in the house.

"Maybe they're not coming back," I said.

"Don't be silly."

"So where are they?"

Clara walked softly to the stairs and peered up. She waved me over. There was a faint light in the hallway. "Could something have happened?" she whispered. The stairs were covered with thick pile carpeting and very steep. "Let's go," I said but Clara shook me off and started up, holding tight to the wooden railing. At the top, we could see that the light, obviously a night light, was coming from the bedroom. The door was half open. For a moment we searched each other's face, then, jerking her arm away, Clara went down the hall. I came up behind her. Bob and Nan lay close together in the brass bed, the covers pulled up over their shoulders, their heads sunk in big white pillows. Next to them was the baby's crib. One of Scotty's fists stuck out between the blue and white bars. He slept with his face turned toward his parents. I watched Clara cover her mouth, more than anything as if she didn't want to infect the room.

Wild Man

Julie was holding her hands like hooks. "All the time I ask myself, where are the passionate people anymore? Where are the risk takers?"

Russell worked a finger under the eye patch and wiped away a line of sweat. The cafe was a little warm. "I know what you mean," he said.

They'd been talking for more than an hour, ever since Julie, a svelte young blonde who'd been staring at him from a nearby table, walked over and asked, already pulling out a chair, "Mind if I join you?", and Russell answered with a suavity he didn't know he possessed, "Not in the least."

"Like my ex, Gerald," Julie went on. "He never wanted to do anything, never wanted to try anything. Gerald was one of those people who won't go on any rides at the amusement park. Literally. He never got over his father taking him on a roller coaster when he was six. After that you couldn't get him on the bump cars." She poured cream into her third cup of Hawaiian blue mountain. Russell was still nursing his second mocha latte. Ordinarily, he would have switched to something decaffeinated by now, but he was afraid of how that would look. "Don't get me wrong. Gerald was a nice man. Sensitive. I like sensitive. But I think you can overdo that."

"You definitely can."

"I'd say you're probably pretty sensitive yourself. But not in a bad way. You've got some edge to you. Mind passing the sugar?"

"Not in the least."

Still adjusting to the reduction in his peripheral vision, he turned his body with care. Last Saturday he'd driven to the Drug Palace in Silver Spring in order to get out of the apartment and be among people. The public library closed early on weekends and he'd seen every movie in town. He'd strolled the aisles of the emporium with a wire basket, occasionally dropping things in. He'd just entered the personal care aisle when he spotted some eye patches in little dust-covered boxes, arranged on the shelf like fallen dominoes. He put one in his basket and moved on. Later, standing before his bathroom mirror, he stretched the nylon cord above his head and settled the piece of black leather over his left eye. He struck various poses. In the days that followed, he was even more impatient than usual to leave work. (He was a proof reader for a textbook company. Julie was part owner and manager of Cinderellarobics, an exercise spa in the Dupont Circle area.) He couldn't wait to get home and put on the eye patch. He wore it right up until bedtime, catching glimpses of himself in the hall mirror, his wine glass, the TV set, and other reflective surfaces. This morning, a cool Saturday in mid-October, he made the half hour trip into D.C., parking his green Neon on busy Wisconsin Avenue in Georgetown. With the aid of the rearview mirror, he slipped on the eye patch, then stepped out onto the pavement. Instantly he noticed the appraising glances of an attractive redhead across the street. As he strode down the sidewalk both men and women gave him the once-over. In his eagerness to begin the day he'd skipped breakfast. Normally he disliked eating alone in public, but when he came to Javaland, a well known hot spot on M Street, he went right in. All heads turned his way.

"It got so the only thing Gerald wanted to do was lounge around the apartment," Julie said as she dumped sugar in. "Reading books and listening to music."

"That gets old."

"Very." She took a big sip of her coffee. "So tell me Russ, what do you like to do besides tennis and horse back riding?"

Earlier, he'd exaggerated his athletic prowess. Should they end up seeing more of each other, he hoped they wouldn't get around to anything equestrian. He hadn't been on a horse since he was a boy and still recalled with some vividness sitting atop the giant, unsteady animal with only the thin, slack reins to hold on to.

"I jog sometimes," he said. "Run, I mean."

"Ever been in a marathon?"

"No. Have you?"

She nodded. "I do the Marine marathon every year. I recently finished in the top hundred for the first time."

"Congratulations."

"What about white-water rafting? Ever done that?"

"No. But I've always wanted to." Nor was he crazy about the water. But at least he knew how to swim. And if worse came to worse, he could always wear one of those orange life preservers. "Actually," he said, "I've been looking for a new challenge."

"Give it a try. You'll love it."

He caught a whiff of Julie's perfume. It wasn't that bone-dry, evanescent stuff Katrina went in for; this was bold and direct, like Julie herself. Russell couldn't remember a woman ever coming on to him in this overt fashion. And so young too, somewhere in her late twenties, at least ten years Russell's junior. He was well aware of the law of mutual attractiveness, of all the rejecting and rejection that goes on before you find yourself with someone of exactly equal desirability. Any hope of appealing to a woman of Julie's caliber had been knocked out of him before he finished high school.

"By the way," Julie said. "What happened?" She touched her left eye. "I hope you don't mind my asking."

"Not at all. Hunting accident."

"You hunt?"

"When I was a kid. A gang of us had all these homemade weapons. We used them to kill chipmunks, gophers, anything that moved. A zip gun blew up in my face."

"You must have been pretty wild, huh?"

"Well."

"I like it. I like the way it looks. I hope that's OK. It gives you this air of intrigue. There's so little of that around these days."

Julie crossed her long, tanned legs, her red leather mini-skirt squeaking. He imagined inserting his hand between the firm thighs. He could almost feel the ripple of muscle under his palm, the warm pressure, the tight plushy fit. "You have no self-pity about it, do you?" Julie said.

"About what?"

"Your eye."

"Oh. No. I guess not."

"Gerald was always complaining about something. A real whiner, you know. I hated that. I like people with spirit. Sometimes I think I have too much. Gerald thought I did."

"I like your spirit."

"Do you?"

"Very much."

"That's nice. You say things straight out, don't you? You don't bullshit a person."

"I try not to." Russell asked Julie if she'd like another coffee.

"No thanks. But you know what I would like? You doing anything after this?"

"I'm free the rest of the day."

"Great. How about grabbing brunch somewhere? I'm starving. They have a fabulous buffet over at the Westin."

"I'd love that." He insisted on picking up the tab and waved the waitress over with his Visa card.

Since Julie had walked to Javaland from her apartment, they took Russell's car. Driving with the eye patch wasn't all that difficult, though he would have probably benefited from more experience. It was hard to resist glancing over his shoulder every few seconds; and he had a tendency to turn his head far to the left, eyeballing the road in front of him.

At the hotel restaurant they filled their plates at the buffet table and arranged themselves side by side in one of the oversized booths. There was an embarrassing moment when Russell, after setting his tray down, swept the salt and pepper shakers onto the floor, but they'd moved quickly past it.

"What about you, Russ?" Julie said between bites of her Spanish omelet. "Ever been married?"

Russell had some gentlemanly scruple about discussing old loves, but he didn't see anything wrong with speaking in general terms about his women, especially since they were all the same: nervous and high strung, always on the brink of crisis or breakdown, women hostage to their own overly refined sensibilities, women very much like himself.

"No, but I've dated quite a lot. Mostly women of the artistic temperament."

"Ugh. The worst."

Russell finished chewing a forkful of blueberry pancakes and swallowed. "Yes. Although they can be fun. At least at first."

"Oh, I know. They're always having deep thoughts and making observations and being perceptive all over the place. Nothing escapes their attention–except the moment. They're never in the moment. Gerald was a head man all the way. All thought, no action. Which screws a person up, don't you think?"

"Absolutely."

"What got me about Gerald, what burned my ass, was that he was so into his own maladjustment, his own fucked-upness."

Russell decided one anecdote about Katrina wouldn't hurt. "This one woman I went out with... sometimes she refused to let me talk to her because my breathing bothered her, that little intake of air just before you speak. Once she noticed it, she said, she couldn't stop hearing it. She even wrote a poem about it. 'Gasp' it was called."

"That's what I'm talking about. That's it exactly. I've sworn off those types forever."

"Me, too."

He considered what sex with Julie would be like: uninhibited, non-stop, a little dirty–wild, as she might say. Even when he and Katrina did manage to have sex, it usually ended badly, Katrina running out to the car and sobbing in the front seat for half an hour (incest taboo: she and her bother had been close during their teenage years).

Julie leaned forward. "Mind if I touch it?"

Before he could answer she'd brushed the eye patch's soft leather with her fingertips. Her nails were painted fire engine red. Her other hand was on his knee.

"What's under there anyway? It's not like a hole or anything is it?"

He'd been fearing this question. Sooner or later, if things worked out, she'd have to see for herself. Looks perfectly normal, would have covered him, but he decided to postpone that moment until she knew him...maybe loved him. He'd take that chance.

"No," he said, "but it's not pretty."

She sat back in the booth, studying him. "I'll be right up front with you, Russ. I've really enjoyed being with you this morning."

"I've enjoyed being with you, too."

"And I'd really like to see you again."

"I was thinking the same thing."

"But I don't think we're the kind of people for the conventional dating bit, do you? A movie and dinner and I'll-call-you-next-week. That's not our style."

"No."

"We need something a little more...us."

"We do."

"Have you ever done any skydiving?"

"No."

"Neither have I. Which is why it excites me. I've already talked to the guy who runs one of the skydiving clubs here in town. It's a hundred and twenty-five dollars a jump. That sounds like a lot, I know, but it's different from most clubs where the instructor jumps with you, piggy-back style. In this one he takes you up to ten thousand feet and lets you go. You jump alone, free fall for a full minute, then pull your own rip cord."

"Maybe we could do that sometime."

"How about this afternoon?"

"This afternoon?"

"You said you were free. The jump site's only two hours away. All you need is a helmet and a pair of boots."

"I have neither, I'm afraid."

"You can borrow Gerald's boots. He left a lot of his junk when he moved out. And I have an extra helmet you can borrow. I was really into trail bikes once."

"Don't we have to go through a period of instruction first?"

"This guy offers a training session every Saturday at two. We can make it if we hurry. The cost of the session is included in the jump fee."

"I don't have that much cash on hand, unfortunately."

"No problem. He accepts all major credit cards."

The man or woman, he couldn't tell which, had been falling for a good sixty seconds. He or she had started out as a speck trailing away from the silver plane like a tiny turd. Several more seconds went by. The parachute still hadn't opened. At what seemed the last possible moment, a streamer of white silk unfurled above the jumper's head and the body jerked to an upright position. The woman, it turned out, landed in a distant corner of the field, after barely missing some telephone wires.

"I hate this waiting," Julie said.

Russell tried to speak but no words came out.

"Now the wind's picking up again." The windsock beside the hangar was fully engorged, which meant another delay, the third one that afternoon. "If this keeps up we won't get to jump at all today."

"Don't even say that," Russell managed. He nudged at the hard ground with the toe of Gerald's black leather boot. He was also wearing Gerald's coveralls, khaki-colored and as comfortable as a pair of old pajamas.

"Be right back," Julie said.

Russell hurried around to the little toilet inside the hangar. He urinated for the fourth or fifth time since their arrival. After stopping by Julie's spacious apartment, with its panoramic view of Northern Virginia (all Russell could see out the window of his Tacoma Park efficiency was the back of a Chinese restaurant), they had changed clothes and sped off in Julie's Mazda. Russell had been relieved when Julie offered to take her car, but her driving rattled his nerves, already on edge. She'd switched lanes constantly, passed everything in sight, flashed her headlights at slower vehicles, all the while talking over a blaring radio. He hadn't minded, though, when she said, "I've been giving your job situation some thought. We're overstaffed at Cinderellarobics, but I know someone in the business who's looking for a male fitness instructor. I'd be happy to put in a good word for you." He'd told her at brunch how much he hated his job at the textbook company, careful to avoid any whining. "A person of your natural athleticism should fit right in," she said. "It's full time, great benefits, and somewhere in the thirty-five thousand range to start."

Thirty-five thousand dollars! Ten thousand more than he was making now. He could get a decent apartment. He could pay off his debts. More important, he'd have a job he wasn't ashamed of, something with a future. "I'll think about it," he said coolly. For that instant he'd forgotten where they were bound.

The jump site, it so happened, was somewhere in western Maryland, a rocky field bordering farm land and a sparse line of trees. The lone airplane hangar was a large, makeshift structure at the end of a narrow runway. They'd gotten there just as the training session was starting. Ed, their jump instructor, a burly ex-Marine, had lectured the dozen new members on exiting the plane, how to free fall without rolling, when to pull the rip cord and the proper landing techniques. He'd spoken for all of twenty minutes. He might have been giving them tips on changing a tire.

Russell zipped and went back outside. Though the sun was warm on his face, he was shivering and stuck his hands deep in his pockets.

Carlos, another new club member, sidled up beside him. "Thirty-six."

"What?"

"That's how many people died last year doing this. I looked it up." A short wiry man with wavy black hair, Carlos held a burning cigarette in one hand, a canary yellow motorcycle helmet in the other. "I keep telling myself I can just leave." He sucked on his cigarette. "So why don't I?"

Russell didn't need to be hearing this, but he couldn't think of how to get away. "I'm a little nervous myself," he said.

"I've had nightmares about jumping and I haven't even done it yet."

"Your chute won't open?"

"Worse. I've jumped without one. I go to pull the rip cord but all I've got is a handful of shirt. You want to hear something hilarious? I'm afraid of heights. I don't even like to get up on a ladder to change a light bulb." He took another drag. "Soon we're going to be hurtling toward the earth at a hundred miles an hour. One minute of free fall. Do you know how long a minute can be?" He peered at Russell. "You're not hearing this, are you? You're not even fazed. That's because you're one of these daredevils. I've noticed that. Except for a few cowards like myself, most of the people here have done stuff like this before: kayaking, scuba diving, mountain climbing. Dangerous stuff. Crazy stuff. This attracts a certain breed. You're one of them. You belong here."

"You don't have to free fall for the whole minute," Russell said. "You can always pull your rip cord right after leaving the plane."

Carlos let his cigarette fall to the ground and stamped on it. "I've thought of that. But imagine how it would look. Pretty squirrelly. You might as well not jump if you're going to do that." Then he asked, looking pointedly at the left side of Russell's face, "You get that in some war? You're a vet, right?"

"No."

"I was sure you were."

"Hunting accident," Russell said.

"Big game?"

He told Carlos the zip gun story.

"There it is. That's exactly what I was saying. You're barely out of kindergarten and you're getting into scrapes, raising hell. Me, I'm reading comic books under the covers with a flashlight. God, I envy that."

They were quiet a moment as they watched Julie talking to Ed on the runway.

"Is she a model or something?" Carlos asked.

"Something."

"You two married?"

"No."

"But you're a couple. I don't mean to pry. You don't see a woman like that every day, that's all." Carlos got so close their shoulders touched. "Mind if I tell you something?"

"I suppose not."

"I haven't had a date in six years."

There was an awkward silence. Finally Russell said, "I'm sorry."

"That's why I'm doing this, to be perfectly honest. I figure it this way: Even if I only jump this one time, it's something I can work into conversations with women. It'll make an impressive ice breaker."

Julie was coming toward them now. Her orange jump suit was stretched tight across her hips and shoulders. She'd left the two top buttons undone.

"Ed doesn't know if we'll be able to get our jumps in today," she told them. "It's wait and see."

"Damn," Russell said.

Julie linked her arm in Russell's. To mask his shivering, he crossed his ankles and held his other arm rigidly against his leg.

Carlos stooped down and picked some blades of grass. He let the wind take them. They blew sharply to the right. "That's us at ten thousand feet."

Julie pushed back her sleeve, revealing a black sport's watch, and proceeded to take Carlos' pulse.

"What is it?"

"One ten."

She stepped over to Russell.

"Why bother? The man's got ice water in his veins."

When she was finished she said to him, "It's a little high."

"It's always like that. It runs in my family, rapid pulse rates."

She looked at him and smiled. "OK."

At Julie's suggestion, she and Russell went for a walk. Hugging herself, Julie stared at the ground in front of her. She'd pulled her hair back in a pony tail, exposing her long neck and small pink ears. "I'm so glad we're doing this together, aren't you? I know we just met, but I have a good feeling about it."

"I–" Russell tripped and fell.

"Are you all right?" She helped him up.

"Fine. Thank you."

"What were you going to say?"

"I have a good feeling about it, too."

"Do you believe in fate?"

"Yes. I think so."

She linked her arm in his again. "I didn't tell you this before, but I've been living in that neighborhood for three years and this morning was the first time I'd ever set foot in Javaland."

"Me, too. Quite a coincidence."

"No. I don't believe in coincidences. I think everything happens for a reason. Both of us being there today, that was no accident." They stopped under a tall, leafless oak. "I've been looking for a certain kind of man for a long time, Russ. I thought Gerald was that man, but I couldn't have been more wrong. The ignorance of youth, I guess. But now...now I think I may have found him. And just two blocks from my apartment." She put her arms around his neck and kissed him hard on the mouth. "You're trembling," she said and moved her hands up and down his back. "That's so damn flattering. I love your passion. We're going to have a lot of fun together. Be patient. You'll see."

It was getting on toward dusk when the windsock began to sag. Ed told all those who still wanted to jump to get ready—at a slight additional risk, he cautioned, given the unpredictable wind conditions combined with the waning sunlight.

The parachute was heavier than Russell imagined. He had to lean forward whenever he wanted to walk. A square handle was attached to the front; pulling on it activated the main chute. A much smaller one, about the size of a key ring, released the reserve chute. He practiced reaching for the handles without looking. A car started up in the parking lot. Hunched over the steering wheel, Carlos turned onto the access road and, accelerating, sent up a cloud of dust.

"Loser," Julie said.

Russell strapped on his helmet. Along with Ed and Julie and two other new members, he climbed into the body of the plane. They sat cross-legged on the thinly carpeted floor. Ed faced them in the little jump seat behind the pilot. Sliding the door shut, he tapped the pilot's shoulder and the engine started with a roar. The plane taxied down the runway, picked up speed and leapt into the air. There was a small window on either side of the plane and Russell watched as the ground fell away. Seconds later he could discern the curvature of the earth. Julie gave him a thumbs up.

The plane continued to climb. After a few minutes of flight it leveled off and Ed slid the door open. Cold air whipped through the cabin. A silver-helmeted man who couldn't have been more than twenty, a boy really, volunteered to go first. With Ed's assistance he moved out onto the strut. Ed signaled the pilot who cut the engine. It sputtered and the plane slowed. "Go!" Ed hollered. The boy sprang away from the plane. Russell chose not to watch the next jumper.

Julie turned to him and shouted over the wind and the engine noise, "Mind if I go ahead?"

He shouted back, "Not in the least."

Getting to her feet, she gave his helmet a pat. "See you on the ground." He didn't watch Julie jump either.

Ed, framed in the doorway by a purplish sky, was beckoning him. With his combat boots, stocking cap and thick jacket, the jump instructor looked like a polar explorer, one of those in old photographs taken on the eve of his disappearing forever down a crevasse. Willing one heavy boot in front of the other, Russell made his way to the door.

"Remember," Ed hollered through cupped hands. "Count to sixty and pull."

Russell moved to the edge, reached out and grabbed hold of the bar attached to the underside of the wing. Ed held his elbow as he moved out onto the little step that jutted a foot or so from the plane.

"Ready?" Ed said.

Russell didn't respond.

Ed shouted, "Ready?"

Russell nodded and Ed signaled the pilot. The engine sputtered, the plane slowed.

"Go! *Go!*"

Russell flexed his knees. The wind was pushing hard against the whole length of his body. He felt like he was being forced off a ledge.

He let go.

It was like every falling dream he'd ever had, a no-turning-back, lead-weight, earth-sucking plunge of stupefying horror and certain death. He opened his mouth to scream but nothing came out. He fought the instinct to curl into a ball. He was tilting backwards. Suddenly he was on his back. He was fumbling for the rip cord when his body rolled over and the ground reappeared. As instructed, he flung out his arms and spread his legs, finally stabilizing himself. The wind whooshed and pounded in his ears. His coveralls snapped like a flag in a hurricane. He started to roll again. He'd forgotten to count to sixty. He'd forgotten to count at all. He pulled the rip cord.

Instantly, he felt the sensation of being yanked back up into the sky. This was replaced by a feeling of being suspended, of being hung up in mid-air. It was hard to believe he was losing altitude. Below and to his right, he could see the tin-roofed hangar, the runway strip and the other jumpers, their tiny white parachutes suggestive of airborne mushrooms. He kept expecting the distance between him and other jumpers to close. Instead, he seemed to be moving farther away. Caught in some updraft or crosswind, he was being carried in another direction, drifting over trees, telephone wires, a blacktop road, then a huge field with a wooden fence running through it. The ground was rushing up at him now. His angle of descent put him in a direct line with the fence. Transfixed, he braced for a collision. But he was dropping faster than he realized and fell short, barely missing some rocks, landing hard–too hard–his body collapsing and tumbling.

As soon as he tried to stand he felt the pain in his big toe. He'd also forgotten he was supposed to turn against the wind just before landing. Wincing with each step, he collected his parachute and removed his helmet, rolling the silky material around it. After getting his bearings, he set off with a heavy limp. Moments later, hobbling through a wooded area, he heard his name being called. Farther on, he made out several figures moving in his direction through a narrow clearing, Julie in the lead, her orange jump suit glowing faintly in the darkening glade. He was raising his hand–then he wasn't. He slapped at his face. He picked at his clothing. Squatting, he patted the earth all around him. It was hopeless. In the failing light, even had the eye patch fallen near by, it would have been impossible to find. He stood up. Shivering again, he clinched his teeth to keep them from chattering. The search party was still calling his name; they hadn't spotted him yet. Crouching low, he took a step backwards, then another. He slipped behind a tree and pressed his back against it. They were so close now he could hear the crunch of leaves underfoot. He slid to the base of the tree. He hunkered down.

Moving Away

I heard the van before I actually saw it, a creaking black and yellow truck with a dented fender, chipped paint and a single windshield wiper flailing at a mist of fine rain. I noted there were only two men in the cabin. I had asked for three. I had told the woman I was willing to pay extra for a third man. "Excellent," she'd said. Perhaps he was curled up in the back on those pads they use, I thought, making the best of the dark, bumpy ride.

I stepped into the street, waving my umbrella.

The van came to a bucking, rattling halt. "This 1804 California?" the driver asked.

I nodded, then introduced myself.

He was Jimmy, the driver said and that, pointing with his thumb at the large man beside him, that was Rollo.

"Shall we begin?" I said.

"Not yet. First we got to discuss terms. We'll park and come up."

"Excellent," I said.

I rode with them in the elevator. I felt somewhat reassured by their identical navy blue sweatshirts, District Movers stenciled across the chest, and their matching caps. They looked official. District had the lowest rates of all the moving companies I'd called. I worried they might be fly-by-night, although not enough to check with the Better Business Bureau, which Annie said I might want to do, but without pressing me. It was my ball game. Normally Annie handled the business end of things. Once she'd convinced me we should buy a condominium, she'd contacted a real estate agent, looked at apartments, applied for a loan–all that. But the other week she blew up at me. We were in this together yet I was content to let her do everything, as usual, to let her shoulder all the responsibility. She was tired of it. Ashamed, for of course she was right, I agreed to be the one to deal with the movers. Besides, she added, it was a man's job.

"You got a freight elevator?" Jimmy said.

"I'm afraid not."

"This one's kind of small."

"I know," I said with feeling, as if it were my perpetual complaint about the building. I noted the muscular upper body on both men, Rollo especially, who was a foot taller than Jimmy. He stood at the back of the elevator, shoulders hunched, arms dangling, his big hands cupped and turned in.

"Too bad about the rain," I said.

"Nah," Jimmy said. He turned and feigned a punch to Rollo's midsection, then followed with a blow to his forearm. "Perfect day for a move, eh man?"

Rollo broke into a slow grin. "Hey," he said.

I led them through the apartment, Jimmy jotting down figures on a clipboard, Rollo shuffling close behind. When we returned to the living room to sign the contract, Annie was sitting on a stack of boxes in the doorway.

Jimmy wetted his pencil with the tip of his tongue. "This everything?"

"There's one more..." Annie and I had spoken at the same time. Jimmy looked around at each of us.

"He'll tell you," Annie said and sat back.

"There's one more piece of furniture," I explained. "In the apartment next door. A cabinet." For as long as I could remember Annie had talked about collecting antiques, and just yesterday, in honor of our new home, as she referred to the condominium, she had purchased from our neighbor a Mission Oak cabinet, circa 1890.

"We'll be sure and leave room in the truck," Jimmy said. He slapped the pencil against the clipboard. "Okay. Two ways we can go here: flat rate or hourly rate. This being a three-man job, hourly's fifty dollars."

I asked how long it would take, approximately. I was asking Rollo, figuring the big man would be more likely to give an honest answer. Rollo's slack features began to switch on, but before he could speak Jimmy said, "Four to five hours."

I didn't hesitate. "I'd prefer the flat rate then."

"He'd prefer the flat rate. What does he bid?"

I calculated quickly. A two-man job, I recalled, cost thirty-five dollars an hour, but since, as Jimmy intimated, a third man did in fact exist, I would be shelling out at least two hundred, probably more.

"One seventy-five."

Jimmy passed his hand over his face, then shot me a look, as though my negotiating prowess had caught him off guard. He glanced down at his clipboard. "Two twenty-five."

"Two hundred," I countered.

Jimmy scratched up under his cap. He looked back at me. "All right. You got me."

Annie was on her feet, smiling

Jimmy shook his head at her. "Drives a hard bargain, don't he?"

"He does," Annie said. "He does."

From the dining room window, we watched the movers load the van. It was still raining. Annie said she was impressed with Jimmy's and Rollo's professionalism: they had covered all the furniture with plastic and taken their time with the more fragile items. She said, too, slipping her arm through mine, that it was odd, total strangers handling our personal belongings. I patted her arm but continued my vigil. Several times in the movers' comings and goings I thought I'd spotted someone of medium height and build I hadn't seen before, only to have him turn out, after closer examination, to be either Jimmy or Rollo. I decided now that the third man must be a behind-the-scenes type who never left the back of the van, his primary function being arranging and stacking things in order to maximize space. Annie must have come to the same conclusion. Otherwise, she would have said something. But no, I'd forgotten. I was in charge and Annie, having relinquished command, was viewing everything as a mere spectator, as I would have done normally. Just then I felt Annie's arm encircle my waist. What's this? I thought.

"I can't say I'm going to miss this place," she said.

"You've always hated it here."

"Because it felt temporary."

"Five years," I said.

"I know," she sighed. "But I'm sure we're doing the right thing, buying. It's foolish to go on paying the rent we're paying when for a little more each month we can have our own place."

"A lot more," I said, and frowned.

She kissed me quickly on the cheek. "Grumpers."

How long had it been since she called me that? "All I'm saying is, for five years—"

"Grumpers grumpers grumpers." She rested her head on my shoulder. "Say. Know what we should do, once we're in over there, soon as the movers have gone–first thing?"

"Spray?"

"No, silly. Before that. Before everything."

"Oh," I said. I couldn't believe it.

"It's been a while, you'll admit."

"It has." I'd thought that was finally over with between us. Nothing had been said, we seldom talked openly about those things, but I'd assumed, after this latest and longest respite, that she felt the same way I did.

"It'll go better," she said, "in the new place. Here, I don't know. I've been too depressed. We need this change, Phillip. The relationship needs it." I felt her fingers snaking over my scalp. "You'll see."

Annie remembered we hadn't had any breakfast and suggested we grab a quick bite at Chick'n Bucket. I wasn't that hungry. I had one piece of chicken, which I ate too fast, burning the roof of my mouth, and nibbled at my cole slaw and french fries. Annie finished all of hers then what was left of mine. She mentioned taking some chicken back for the movers, but I was afraid that if they ate now they might lose momentum. "I would have never thought of that," she said, reached over the paper plates and squeezed my hand. When we got back the living room was still full of boxes. For something to do, as well as to take my mind of Annie's revived amorousness, I began carrying the cartons of books into the hallway. I held the elevator door open as Rollo stacked them inside. It was going on three hours now and I had to congratulate myself for choosing the flat rate. Yes, the elevator was too small and, yes, there was a lot to move, but as Jimmy himself had said, it was a three-man job. Jimmy sent Rollo down alone on the elevator and, a little winded, said, "That cabinet."

I went to get Annie, who had borrowed a key to Mrs. Talbott's apartment.

I was seeing the cabinet for the first time. It was an antique all right, constructed of solid dark-stained oak with brass handles and numerous plates of glass. It put most of our other furniture to shame.

"I didn't expect nothing like this," was Jimmy's comment. "This could cost a little extra."

"How much extra?" Annie said. She put her fist to her mouth.

"How much extra?" I said.

"You see this?" Jimmy ran his fingers along the back of the cabinet. "It's loose." I saw where the back piece had separated slightly down one side. A few nails were visible. "And there's all this glass."

"It's an antique," I said.

"That's what I know, I know that—now. You didn't mention it before."

Rollo entered the room. He walked over to the cabinet, grabbed hold and began pulling on it. Jimmy clapped him hard on the back, so I hard I jumped. The big man stood up, confused, and then glared. Ignoring Rollo's dark looks, Jimmy said, "You didn't mention this was some antique."

"But you've been moving antiques—well, old and valuable furniture—all morning," I said. "This one just happens to be in a different apartment." I had an idea. "Look. I'll tell you what. It's getting late. I'm sure you're both pretty hungry. We'll spring for your lunch, burgers or something, and call it even. How does that sound to you?"

Jimmy removed his cap and stood with his hands on his hips. He looked at Annie. "He's tough. I said it before. Another one for you, general."

Jimmy positioned himself at one end of the cabinet. He beckoned Rollo, who, sulking and seemingly intransigent, looked on. Jimmy took a deep breath, as though his patience were exhausted, and said to Rollo, "Now we take it. Ready?..Set?..." Perversely, I was a little disappointed when Rollo, after a brief hesitation, caved in and shuffled over to his end.

I followed them down. Outside, I permitted Jimmy to talk me into lending a hand. The cabinet *was* heavy. Together we pushed it up the ramp and into the truck where a space had been made just inside the door. Rollo jumped down and disappeared, leaving Jimmy to close up the van.

"By the way," I said. "What would you like on your burgers?"

"Everything," Jimmy said.

"Well, that's easy." I handed him a map I'd drawn up with directions to the new place. It wasn't far but I didn't want to take any chances. Jimmy glanced at it, then tried to give it back. "It's yours," I said. Jimmy shrugged and stuffed it in his pocket.

"So," I said. "We'll stop by this Wendy's over here and meet you at the loading dock in like fifteen minutes." I decided it was time I said something. "Oh, yeah. I still haven't seen that third man. I'm guessing he was detained. Can I assume he'll be catching up with you at the new address?"

Jimmy smiled. "Yeah," he said. "You can assume that."

"You're handling everything beautifully," Annie said. We were walking through the new apartment, the creaking floorboards echoing in the empty rooms. "I'm so proud of you."

I followed her aimlessly into the bedroom. Larger than the one on California Street, it had a ten foot high ceiling, built-in bookcases and a walk-in closet.

"We're going to love it here," she said. "I know it." She pulled the Venetian blind and opened the window. The rain had stopped and the sun broken through. Annie stood looking out, the light revealing the curve of her breast. I recalled what would soon be expected of me. "Come see," she said and waved me over, groped for my hand.

In the park below a young woman was pushing two swings at the same time, a little girl in one, an even smaller boy in the other. The woman ran back and forth, giving each child a hard shove, putting all her weight behind it, causing the children to scream loudly and crazily.

"My God," I said, thinking the children were being terrorized by some mad woman.

"What is it?"

Then I realized they were merely laughing. "Nothing," I said. "Really."

Annie closed the window, reached up and knocked on the wall. "Feel how thick."

Obediently I rapped with my knuckle.

"We can make all the noise we want," she said.

I said I should be getting down to the loading dock, that there was something I needed to check on. Roaches had been a big problem in the old apartment and as a preventive measure Annie was sprinkling boric acid along the baseboards. I left her bent over in the corner, tapping the powder out of the can. At the end of a long corridor I turned right, then left. I realized I was lost (the place was cavernous), backtracked, got lost again and only found my way after coaxing complicated directions from an elderly woman I met at the mail chute. I got to the loading dock in time to see Rollo leaving the van, a half dozen lamps cradled in his arms, cords hanging down to his ankles. He tripped or lost his footing and one of the lamps toppled to the pavement. He stepped on the shade.

Jimmy dashed over. "You broke the man's lamp," he shouted. Rollo set the other lamps aside and withdrew his foot from the mangled wire frame.

"He didn't, actually," I said, happy for Rollo's sake but disappointed otherwise. If the lamp had been smashed, it might have put Annie out of the mood she was in. "The lamp itself is undamaged."

"Broke it real good," Jimmy went on.

"Honestly, that shade was worthless, a piece of junk. He's done us a favor." This was true. Annie had spoken often about replacing the shade and would be pleased to hear of its destruction. The lamp was another matter: a pseudo-antique, it had been a gift from a favorite aunt and held great sentimental value for her. I moved my hands over the porcelain. It seemed incredible to me that something so fragile could have struck concrete and remained intact.

"Won't happen again," Jimmy said. "You got my word on it. Somethin' like this happens again—" (he sliced the air) "no tip. Won't expect it, won't accept it. And you," he said, pointing a finger at Rollo. "I'm watching you. I got my eye on you."

I thought that now, surely, Jimmy had gone too far, but Rollo just stood there, taking it. I couldn't decide which man I was angrier at, Jimmy for being such a bully, or Rollo for letting him. I snatched up one of the lighter boxes and carried it to the elevator.

When they started bringing stuff into the apartment, Annie was standing in the living room. She noted each item, pointing in the direction of the appropriate room.

"Man's a slave driver," Jimmy said.

When they were ready to go down for the next load, I told them to go on ahead, that I'd be along shortly.

"You hear that, Rollo?" Jimmy said. "He's not coming. Maybe now we can catch our breath." He placed a conciliatory hand on Rollo's shoulder. I was watching carefully. The big man didn't actively remove it but he did walk quickly away, slipping out from under Jimmy's grasp. I was glad to see Rollo wasn't completely lacking in backbone.

"There are a few things I think you should know," I said, trailing Annie into the kitchen. "For one, I'm the third man. You're looking at the third man."

"I know," she said. "Help me open this, will you?"

I ripped the tape off a large cardboard box. "But can you believe it?"

"Don't let it upset you." She unwrapped some dishes covered with newspaper and set them in the sink. "I mean, we're getting such a good price. It's been hours. Deciding on the flat rate, all that haggling you did–that was so smart of you."

"Something else. Something I just found out. Are you ready for this? They're expecting a tip. I've never heard of movers getting a tip, have you? They practically demanded it."

"So give them a few dollars." She laughed. "I think they're cute."

I couldn't understand it. Annie should have been outraged by all this, even if she wasn't the one in charge, just as her aunt's lamp should have shattered into a million pieces.

"Another thing. They dropped your lamp. You know the one. It's a miracle it didn't break."

"That must mean good luck." She looked at me. "Are you all right?"

"Of course. Why?"

She didn't answer.

I kicked the box into the corner. Annie wouldn't let me get away without a kiss.

As I was coming off the elevator in the garage I heard laughter and loud talking. Jimmy and Rollo were standing inside the van, empty now except for some of the more cumbersome pieces. They were taking turns slapping each other's upraised palm, hooting uproariously. So much for my hopes of Rollo's independence. After they were done carrying on, Rollo lifted our huge mattress and, balancing it on his head, stepped from the truck.

"My man," Jimmy said to me. "Mind grabbing that end?" Jimmy had pushed the box springs to the edge of the van. Using the flat of his hand, he pounded the springs. "Good action on these babies."

"What?" I said.

"Lotsa bounce." Jimmy chuckled.

"They're relatively new, if that's what you mean."

He pounded them some more. "Sealy Posture-Pedic—queen size." He sang, "Gonna have some fun tonight, oh ba-by."

I set my end of the springs back down and walked out.

Annie was trying to get the light in the closet to come on. A little brusquely, I stepped past her and began fiddling with the bulb.

"It's the socket," I said. "It's loose. You pay—how much?—eighty-five thousand dollars, and this is what you get, loose sockets. We'll have to call an electrician, you know. This isn't a rental. We can't phone down for the engineer anymore. This place we own. We have to pay for everything ourselves—repairs, everything."

"Phillip," Annie said quietly.

I was well aware of the movers in the other room. If they were listening, so much the better. I regarded Annie, standing with her feet together and her hands clasped over her stomach. She reminded me of a finalist in a grade school spelling bee, perplexed and vulnerable. I walked away to the bathroom. I wanted to wash my face, I felt grimy, and turned on the water, or tried to. The knobs were stuck. No, they turned in the opposite direction from those in the old apartment, clockwise. And, I discovered, the water tasted bad. The water was pipey. I considered the effect this would have on my morning coffee, my favorite moment of the day. Forgetting, I gave the knobs a twist. Hot water rushed out of the faucet and sloshed the front of my shirt.

"You're wet," Annie said when I returned to the bedroom.

"It'll dry."

Jimmy was on his knees beside the closet. He had removed some metal plate and was working on the wires. Rollo peered over his shoulder, entranced.

"Try it now," Jimmy said.

Annie pulled the cord. The light came on, as I knew it would. I left as Jimmy was launching into an account of his electrical wizardry. In the living room I looked in vain for somewhere to sit. The place was a mess. It would take days of hard work before it was livable. I leaned back on the arm of the sofa. Across from me was the Mission Oak. It looked different somehow. I inspected it until I saw what the problem was and asked Annie to step into the living room.

I pointed at the cabinet's back panel, showing her where it had separated. "That wasn't like that," I said. "It was, of course, but not to that extent."

"I don't remember. I didn't get a good look at it."

"You bought it," I said. "You bought the thing." I gave the cabinet a shake. It wobbled, more, I was certain, that it did before. "See how unsteady it is?"

Anne glanced nervously down the hall. "We can just hammer that, can't we?"

"It's not that simple. You don't just hammer antiques. We'll have to get someone to fix it, an antique specialist. It won't be cheap." She didn't seem the least bit upset. "Don't you get it? They did something to your cabinet, when they were bringing it up just now, your precious cabinet."

"Are you sure?"

I called down the hallway. "Excuse me. Could you come in here? I think there's a problem."

Jimmy and Rollo filed into the living room. I said, "The cabinet's been damaged. Here."

Jimmy leaned over and touched the panel. "It was like that."

"Yes and no," I said. I made the cabinet wobble. "It's much worse now."

"It did that, man."

"I won't be deducting anything from the original cost," I said. "A contract's a contract. But I won't be adding to it either. I wanted you to know that the damage had not gone unnoticed, that's all."

"Phillip," Annie said.

Jimmy looked at Annie, then back at me. "Shit."

I knew I had him then, knew I'd won. To get your way, all you did was insist a little. It was that easy. "This would have never happened," I said, "if they'd sent the three men I asked for. You said yourself this was a three-man job."

"I said it, and it was. We been here since ten o'clock. We been here all day. They couldn't spare another man. They sent us anyway. They do that."

"But none of that's my fault, is it?"

I removed from my wallet several large bills and handed them to Jimmy. Without bothering to count them, he crammed them into his back pocket.

Just then Rollo took a step towards me. He sputtered a moment, then shouted, "We didn't do nothin' to that cabinet, man!"

Jimmy blocked Rollo with his arm, as if there actually existed a threat of violence.

"I'm not saying you did it on purpose," I said, addressing Jimmy. "Accidents do happen. All I'm saying is, I wish you'd been straight about it."

Jimmy laughed. He looked at Annie and shook his head, as if she had his complete sympathy. Then he turned Rollo towards the door and led him out.

Annie closed the door and came back. She had the same look of schoolgirl befuddlement.

I turned away from her. "You were some help."

"I didn't know what to say. I mean, it doesn't seem that serious to me. I'm sure we can fix it ourselves."

"You didn't support me."

She was quiet for a moment, then touched my arm. "I'm sorry."

"Don't," I said.

She withdrew her hand. It was that easy.

John Picard

Dear Primitiva

Your letter was waiting for me when I got home from the book store yesterday, the familiar pale yellow envelope a welcome sight among the usual stack of bills and other nuisances. In this age of e-mail and instant messaging, Primitiva, a personal letter–handwritten, at that–is a rare and precious thing. I've always treasured our correspondence is what I'm trying to say.

You write that you're up to 70 pounds thanks to all the food you've been receiving through the Foundation. That's so great. A word of advice though: make sure to save anything non-perishable that's left over. You never know when a little stash might come in handy for emergencies and what not. Have you heard anything about returning to school? I can't tell you how angry it makes me when I think of what those soldiers did to your teacher, poor woman. For someone as fond of learning as you are, Primitiva, I know it must be a hardship, your education interrupted and in such a brutal way. Let's hope some brave individual volunteers to take her place before you fall too far behind in your studies.

The big news, of course, is that the cast has finally come off your leg. How wonderful that you won't have to use those horrible crutches anymore, that you can run and play with the other children in the orphanage again. They do good work at that clinic the Foundation sent you to, apparently. It's not your fault the rebels are digging trenches all over the place that children can't see at night, but from now on I hope you'll be more careful when you're out and about. I most humbly accept your thanks for my part in your treatment and recovery, but you give me too much credit, you always have. I feel embarrassed when I think of you taping my picture above your bed. I don't deserve such an honor. After all, if it wasn't me helping you out, it would be some other member of the Foundation. What I mean is, I'm not the saint you've made me out to be.

As you can already see, this letter is different from the others I've written you. I am using words and phrases that may have you scratching your head and leafing through that dog-eared, Spanish-English dictionary of yours. That's because I have something important to tell you, something that requires a range of expression unavailable in simpler language. I am sacrificing clarity for understanding, if that makes any sense.

I've been doing a lot better myself. I have a new perspective (distance) on that relationship with the young woman I told you about, the one I asked to marry me. I did come on pretty strong, I suppose. We'd only known each other a month. But, to be fair to myself, at 43 one becomes very concerned about one's future. And something good came out of the experience. It forced me to take a good hard look at myself. I mean that quite literally. And what I saw, Primitiva, I didn't like: a man who had let himself go, a man who had thickened through the middle and elsewhere, an unattractive man. Not exactly gordo (I believe that's your word for it), but definitely getting there. It's no wonder she turned me down. What woman wants a husband so neglectful of his health and welfare?

Not long after this realization I had a complete physical and learned that my cholesterol was 265, my blood pressure 140 over 90. These are not encouraging numbers, Primitiva. The doctor said that in addition to losing weight I needed to do something about my cardiovascular system or risk shortening my lifespan. I had to take action, before it was too late. I hope to have a wife and children one day. The bachelor's life isn't what it's cracked up to be, after a certain age. But I'm never going to change my single status, not to mention live to a ripe old age, unless I get into better shape. And physical appearance is important, whether we want to admit it or not.

It occurs to me that in a year and a half I've never told you how I came to be your sponsor. In light of the present circumstances, this might be a good time to do that. I was in my doctor's office with strep throat. I had been waiting for almost an hour and there were still two or three people ahead of me. I felt terrible, feverish and unable to swallow without great pain. To pass the time, I flipped through a magazine until I came to an article that interested me. As I was trying to concentrate, my eyes were drawn to a photograph in the upper left hand corner of the page. It was a picture of a little girl with the biggest, saddest eyes you've ever seen. She was very pretty, though not as pretty as you; and younger, no more than six. The writing underneath said she was hungry and had nothing to eat. It urged the reader to become a sponsor for the Rescue the Children Foundation. $37 a month would provide a child with nutritious food and regular medical care, would, in essence, save her life, and others like her. I had looked into those pleading eyes, if only glancingly, hundreds of times before. The photograph was in many magazines then, and still is today. Like most citizens of this fabulously wealthy country I had become blind to all but the most graphic images of war and poverty. You will find this scarcely believable, Primitiva, but viewing such things on TV every night and reading about them in the newspapers and magazines amounts to a form of entertainment here, a way of enlivening our leisure

John Picard

hours. But this time, for some reason, the picture of the starving girl had a powerful effect on me. When I got home, nearly dizzy with fever, I wrote out my first check for $37. I'll never forget how excited I was three weeks later when my sponsor kit arrived, complete with your photograph and personal history and your letter, the first of many.

The collapse of your economic system, the destruction of your cities, the hourly skirmishes among the warring factions: this has been life in your tragic country the last several years. But I know from your touching and spirited letters that before these catastrophes, before you were separated forever from your family, you did all the things common to girls your age. You once wrote me that one of your fondest memories was saving up your coins and going to the market. You would buy sweets, especially chocolates, and maybe some trinket. If your dear mamacita was with you, she would sometimes buy you a scarf or a hair band or, best of all, a dress. Why did she do this? Why did she spend all that money on a new dress, money that even then was hard to come by? Because you looked so pretty in it, naturally. Because she loved you very much, of course. But also because everyone, no matter who, deserves to get something really nice once in a while.

When I was your age what I desired more than anything in the world was a Davy Crockett jacket. They were very popular then. It was made of suede, tan in color, with fringe dangling from the arms and across the front and back. My parents could have bought me one, but they considered it a waste of money, impractical, and continued to give me windbreakers and fur-lined raincoats instead. I have no right to complain, but I didn't have a very happy childhood. It may surprise you, but even with all our advantages many people here do not. I was an only child. Timid and lacking in self-confidence, I had few friends. And I was sick a lot, which can be very isolating (lonely making). Anyway, when my grandmother gave me five hundred dollars to put toward my college education, I begged my parents to let me use part of it to buy a Davy Crockett jacket. I cried and pleaded. I wouldn't let it go. To their credit, they finally gave in. Primitiva, I wore that jacket until it was in tatters. Even after I outgrew it, when my arms stuck several inches out of the sleeves, I couldn't bring myself to throw it away. Do you remember how it felt the first time you put on a new dress? What a lift it gave you? How it made you feel more sure of yourself, more attractive, special? And wasn't it nice how those good feelings revived (came back) every time you put it on? That's how my Davy Crockett jacket made me feel. And that's how I feel about BioFlex.

Recently I turned on my little TV and found myself watching a commercial for something called The BioFlex Home Conditioning System, which is nothing but a fancy name for an exercise machine. The commercial was shot in soft focus, meaning it was all sort of foggy and dream-like. The people in it, the people using the exercise machine, looked like young gods, perfectly proportioned and well cut (good muscles). The narrator's voice was smooth and reassuring. It was all a very slick come-on, in other words. I am no fool, Primitiva. And yet, by the time the commercial was over I'd jotted down the toll-free number.

Four days later there was a loud knock at my front door. It was the UPS man with a huge cardboard box from BioFlex. I had the various parts out of the box and assembled within minutes, and launched into my first workout. I keep my exercise machine right here in the den, where I'm writing this letter. I wish you could see it. It's quite an impressive piece of machinery, though somewhat difficult to describe. Imagine sitting in a very comfortable leather chair. On either side of you, as well as over head, are lots of pulleys and cables. These are attached to handles and grips that you can either pull or push, depending on what muscle group you're working on. The whole thing stands over six feet tall, reaching almost to the ceiling. Upon entering the room one is immediately struck by "...its gleaming chromium steel, its elegant architecture." (I am quoting from the preface to the training manual.) "There is nothing 'random' about the design of BioFlex. Function dictates design, and functions demanded by a perfect form of exercise dictate the design of the BioFlex System."

Now the hard part. I'll give it to you straight, Primitiva: I don't think I can afford both my sponsorship and my exercise machine. It's a matter of simple arithmetic. I owe the manufacturers $1,789 plus taxes, to be paid in monthly installments of $75.50 over a 24 month period. My sponsorship costs me $37 a month, which may not sound like a lot in comparison, but with everything else–bills, rent, utilities–it adds up. Even minus my sponsorship I'm going to feel the pinch. If it makes you feel any better, I am also letting slide some of the other charities and organizations I donate to: Urban Ministry, Amnesty International, PBS, The Firefighters Association. You see, I am a generous man. I do what I can to help out. I would dip into my savings if I had any. $88.12. That's it!

I suppose I could have joined a health club where there are exercise machines galore. But they are all too specialized. You have to use first this one for ten minutes, then that one for ten minutes, and so on. None of them provides a full-body workout in one compact station. And having one right in one's own home greatly increases the chances one will use it. Proof of this is that I have yet to miss a workout. In addition, my attitude toward life and things in general has greatly improved. Even the people at work have commented on my upbeat spirits. I have more energy than I ever thought possible. And I've already lost 10 pounds!

Of course, I could have taken up jogging, which for shoes and running clothes would only cost me a hundred or so. Or I could have spent the same amount on a tennis racket and gotten up matches at the local courts three or four times a week. But to return to the preface: "Over a period of thirty years, while slowly refining the BioFlex system, we gradually became aware of the requirements for a perfect form of exercise. These requirements are,

– Full-range resistance
– Direct resistance
– Balanced resistance
– Omni-variable resistance
– Rotary-form resistance
– Automatically-variable resistance
– Negative-work potential

Conventional exercises provide only one of these absolute requirements (negative-work potential) and thus are NOT full-range exercises, are NOT proper exercises." You see my point?

I realize that compared to you I live in splendor. My apartment is probably as big as the entire orphanage, which, you say, has to accommodate (hold) over fifty children. I have my own bed. I have all the hot water I want. Only a block from where I live there is a store stocked with delicious foods, including the sweets that you're so fond of. Primitiva, all the chocolate you can eat! And yet, by the standards of my own country I am not a rich man. Far from it. Most men my age here are making twice and three times what I am. And they live in a house, a house in one of the better neighborhoods. The assistant manager of a book store isn't exactly a lucrative occupation. Low pay and mediocre benefits typify it. Don't misunderstand me. I'm not complaining. I made my choices. I could have gone to law school, I could have gotten an MBA, I could have made something of myself, financially speaking. But I didn't care about all that. I've always been somewhat idealistic (dreamy). You see, I was heavily influenced by the Sixties. You can't possibly know what that means, but it has to do with valuing the spiritual aspects of life over the material, with refusing to allow money to dominate your life. Believe me, many of my generation have done just that, piling up possessions and money-market funds like there was no tomorrow, while I have contented myself with used cars, second-hand furniture and a little TV, its tin-foil flag flying from the antenna to improve reception. I am not made of stone. I have splurged on the occasional luxury item, a CD player, a leather coat. I make a trip to the beach every two or three years. But there have been no European vacations, and no extravagant purchases. Until now. Until BioFlex.

More than an hour has passed since I wrote the last paragraph. I have just had the most unsettling conversation with the woman at the Rescue the Children Foundation. She demanded to know why I wanted to terminate my sponsorship. I told her it was due to a financial burden. She wanted to know the nature of that burden. I didn't feel that was any of her business and said so. She asked whether this burden predated my sponsorship or was recently incurred. She needed to know, she said, for her records. I confessed to the latter and was treated to a reproachful silence. That's when I told her I intended to resume sponsorship in precisely two years time.

"I'm calling," I said, "because I'd like to know whether it might be possible for another member of the Foundation to assume my sponsorship until I'm able to make payments again."

Unfortunately, I was part of a growing trend, she said. Cancellation of sponsorships was on the rise. New sponsorships had been falling off for the last five years. An arrangement such as I was suggesting wasn't feasible. Besides, she went on, these days new sponsors were being urged to give to countries with more pressing needs. Things were particularly bad in West Africa and the Far East just now.

"Worse," I said, "than half the population without food and water? Civil war? Murdered school teachers?"

"Yes, sir. Much worse."

"What about a grace period? A couple of months free of charge to ease her back into her old way of–you see what I'm saying?"

"Aid is terminated immediately upon notice of cancellation."

"But she's just getting back on her feet."

There was another long silence, and then, "Would you like to reconsider?"

"Well..."

"I'm sure she'd appreciate it."

"I'm sure she would but...it's only two years."

"And until then, sir?"

"You listen here. You listen to me now." I was yelling. Primitiva, I never yell.

The phone went dead.

It might help you to understand my position if you knew more about the benefits I derive from the BioFlex system. I have a new confidence about my body that has translated into a sense of well-being I've never known before. I've yet to approach another woman for a date, but I can already tell I won't bring to the experience the desperation that women find so off-putting. My self-esteem is higher than it's ever been, and though I won't go so far as to say I can have my pick of women—far from it—I do feel it's only a matter of time before I meet the right one, settle into a mature relationship, and begin living the sort of life more suitable to a middle-aged man. My twenty minute workouts are an integral part of my daily routine now. I would do more than twenty minutes but the manual discourages it. I wish I could convey to you how good they make me feel, both while I'm actually exercising, when, after ten minutes, I enter a state of almost unconscious physicality (like floating), and when, immediately afterwards, the endorphins kick in and I enjoy a brief period of total peace and relaxation. I look forward to these workouts. They give my hours away from the bookstore a structure they've been sorely lacking. I like it. I like having it around the apartment, catching glimpses of it when I pass by the den and sometimes, late at night, turning on the light and looking at it one last time before retiring. It makes me happy. It gives me hope.

Twenty-four months, Primitiva. Then the money will begin flowing again, I promise, arriving at the orphanage as regular as clockwork. Do you think you can hold out that long? Surely they have extra food in that place. How do all the other children get by? Do you hate me? It's not asking too much, is it, that I be permitted this one indulgence, after a lifetime of virtual self denial? Considering my life as a whole (low paying job, crummy apartment, social isolation), I think I deserve what amounts to a gift to myself. In more ways than one, it is a move toward health.

It might interest you to know that I've always wanted a daughter. I actually requested a girl when I became a sponsor. Boys are nice, and I'm sure I would love my son, but there's a special bond that exists between a father and daughter. When I think about having a family, I see myself with a little girl.

I assure you, Primitiva, if she is half as bright and pretty as you, I will consider myself a lucky man.

I know that two years sounds like a long time, especially at your age and in your circumstances, and perhaps it is, of course it is. But here's hoping they pass quickly and safely. Please believe me when I say I wish you the very best.

It's been a several days since I wrote anything here. I didn't want to send this until I had something positive to report. Well, it so happens that I've had my eye on this woman who comes into the book store every two or three weeks. For the first time today I struck up a conversation with her, joining her in the mystery aisle and asking if she needed any help. She didn't, but I got her to open up a bit about her favorite writers and then, in a casual way, I invited her out for coffee. She said she had a boyfriend, so that's that. But I think it's a good sign, don't you, that I finally had the self-confidence–and we know where that comes from–to approach her, to start putting myself out there again. And it's not like she's the only attractive woman who frequents the store. There are dozens of them, and they can't all have boyfriends. In other words, Primitiva, despite this disappointment, despite this little setback, things are looking up.

ps: Write soon.

In middle age, Ludwig Wittgenstein, arguably the century's greatest philosopher, set out on a quest to make amends for past behavior he now deemed cruel and reprehensible.

—Ray Monk Wittgenstein:
The Duty of Genius

The Apology

"It's that nice Mr. Wittgenstein again," Eva said. "Are you sure you won't speak with him?" Eva had strict instructions not to let Wittgenstein in the house. He'd already been by once that day, twice the day before.

"Yes, I'm sure."

"He says he used to be your schoolmaster. Why don't you find out what he wants?"

"I know what he wants."

I'd already heard from Karl and Holvag that Wittgenstein had been to their homes, asking to see them, begging their forgiveness. He was going all over Trattenburg, looking up his former pupils, the ones he'd tormented and abused more than two decades ago, prostrating himself in an effort to assuage a late blooming conscience. They'd consented to see him; they'd accepted his apology. I refused. Had they forgotten how he mistreated us? Had they decided to ignore all the times he'd boxed our ears, smacked our hands with rulers, pulled our hair? And what were our crimes that they required such punishments? What did we do that was so terrible? Misspell "Constantinople." Not know what 14 times 12 equals. Fail to use "engender" correctly in a sentence. I didn't care if he was one of the most important men of the age. I didn't care who his family was, or how highly the world regarded him. I wanted nothing to do with this man who terrorized innocent children.

"We all make mistakes when we're young," Eva said.

"He wasn't that young! He was thirty years old. He should have known better—*then*."

Shaking her head, she returned to the front door, cracked it open and spoke for a moment in a low commiserating tone. I heard Wittgenstein thank her for her trouble in that cultured, upper class voice of his, a voice I had heard rise to a shriek because some child didn't know what a diphthong was. A diphthong! Then I heard on the flagstones another familiar sound, the rat-tat-tat of his walking stick.

Eva said,

"He's such a gentleman, your old schoolmaster. So charming, so intelligent."

All the old anger flared.

"You think so? Take a look at this." I stood and pushed the hair back from my forehead.

"What?"

"The scar," I said, tapping my head. "The scar."

"You mean that little red line?"

"Yes. That's a scar. And do you know where that came from? Do you know who did that to me? It was your Mr. Charming, that's who. It was your Mr. Intelligent. It was *Ludwig Wittgenstein.*"

My parents were simple folk. Except for the Bible, there were no books in our little three-room cottage. They knew nothing of music or literature or art—the finer things of life. As far as they were concerned, I would grow up to be a shop keeper like my father, my future a steady, unexamined trudge to the grave.

Then came word that we were getting a new schoolmaster. The first day of school, in walked a short wiry man with a bony face and unruly hair. He wore a beige jacket and a pair of work pants, a very different uniform from the coat and tie favored by his predecessor. Right off, he did an amazing thing. He stepped to the front of the class and sat on the edge of his desk. At that time, such informality in the classroom was unheard of. But he proceeded to do something even more remarkable. He began to whistle. It was a tune, he said, he'd been listening to on his gramophone that morning. I don't know what impressed me more, his whistling ability, which was considerable, or the transcendent beauty of the melody, several bars from Brahms' second symphony, it turned out. I was enraptured. I had never heard anything like it, never knew such sounds existed in this world, and was keenly disappointed when he left off whistling to begin the math lesson.

I was now myself the village schoolmaster. I was eminently qualified, I felt, having learned from example how not to conduct a classroom. My approach to pedagogy was that of a gentle prod mixed with the mild reproof. If my students sometimes got out of line (the collective grumbling at quizzes, the spitball hurled at the blackboard when my back was turned), I tended to overlook it, attributing it to high spirits and youthful rebellion. The commotion was never so great that I wasn't able to complete the day's lesson, granted when test time came around I found myself grading on a very large curve. Better to err on the side of leniency than strictness was my attitude. And my students loved me! They showed this most tellingly perhaps in their coming back years later to visit me and reminisce about their school days, something that would never occur to anyone who had been exposed to Herr Wittgenstein's daily tyranny.

"He's still out there," Eva said, peering through the blinds. I looked for myself. It was now early evening and Wittgenstein was standing just beyond our property line, leaning on his cane and gazing in the direction of the house. That cane! There was nothing wrong with his legs. The cane was an affectation, a pretension in a man who prided himself on having no pretensions. "I think he's waiting for you to ask him in," Eva said.

"He can go right on waiting."

"It's getting dark," she said. "He must be cold. All he has on is that little jacket."

I went back to reading the evening paper.

"And think how hungry he must be. He hasn't eaten all day. Maybe I'll take him some soup."

"Don't you dare. It'll just be that much longer before he goes away."

Eva put her hands on her hips and gave me a stern look. "This is a side of you I've never seen before, Konrad. I always thought of you as someone with a forgiving nature."

"I am. For the most part."

"Well, I'm very disappointed. Okay, he did things to you he shouldn't have. But he's sorry now. He regrets all that."

I told her I didn't want to talk about it.

She stomped off. When she returned, she was wearing her coat and kerchief. "I'll be back later."

"I absolutely forbid you to go out there and—"

"Where do you get off forbidding me anything?" she snapped. "It's Sunday. I'm meeting Carita and Gretchen at the cinema." I'd forgotten that Sunday was her girls' night out. "You see what's happening, don't you? You see what you're turning into."

"I'm not turning into anything."

She left without a goodbye.

For most of my youth I'd been an indifferent student. I had looked on school, learning in general, as drudgery. Herr Wittgenstein changed all that. Now I couldn't wait to get to class in the morning. My parents were baffled by the change, but not displeased. They no longer had to force me to do my homework. I applied myself eagerly to my lessons. Supplementing my assigned reading, I checked books out of the library my teacher had mentioned in class.

My newfound diligence was not motivated by fear, however. I had witnessed the consequences of Wittgenstein's ire. I had seen him take a swipe at this and that student, box some ears, rap a few knuckles, but, I rationalized, they'd had it coming due to their lack of preparation. I believed him to be fair man, if a bit on the snippy side. I studied hard, not to avoid punishment, but rather because a new world had been opened up to me and I wanted to show by dedication to my studies how grateful I was for this gift.

My favorite part of each school day came when Herr Wittgenstein would read to us from the classics, most often Dickens and Tolstoy, writers who, until then, were unknown to me. He would sit on the edge of his desk and, in a loud, emphatic voice, intone long passages from their works. A lot of the words I didn't know and I would get lost during the more literary parts, but just as I'd intuited that the man reading to us possessed a mind of an extraordinary caliber and refinement, and thus worthy of respect, so did I sense that these texts, however difficult in places, were something exceptional and deserving of my full attention.

I was pretty much alone in my thinking. Most of what Wittgenstein read to us went straight over the heads of my classmates. They would make fun of him, imitating his strident, accented voice, as well as his other mannerisms. I would defend him against these calumnies. For this I was called "teacher's pet," even though Wittgenstein had never showed me the slightest favoritism, despite all my efforts to impress him, despite secretly longing for such treatment.

It might not be overstating it to say that I was infatuated with Herr Wittgenstein, that I had what amounted to a cerebral crush, unrequited, but all the more intense for that reason. Like any smitten youth, I wanted to talk about the object of my affection. When I wasn't telling my parents something that Herr Wittgenstein had said or done, I was reading to them sections from *War and Peace* and *Little Dorrit* in a manner crudely imitative of my schoolmaster. I could not control myself. I went so far as to share with my classmates insights into my extra-curricular reading.

"The thing you have to remember about *Tale of Two Cities*," I might say, excitedly, recalling something I'd read in the introduction, "is that it's the only novel in which Dickens moderates his use of irony."

Such observations were met with rolled eyes, accusations of showing off—not altogether untrue—and worse. After I'd had a brand new copy of *Anna Karenina* ripped from hands and stomped into the dirt, I became more restrained in my enthusiasm. Yet I continued to defend my teacher's honor whenever I felt it had been impugned, to identify myself more and more with his way of being.

I see now that I had set myself up for disappointment. I had climbed heedlessly to the summit of schoolboy adoration; some sort of slip was inevitable, followed by a nasty fall.

Indeed, late on a Friday afternoon, I found myself standing rigidly beside my desk, Herr Wittgenstein glaring at me from very close range. Only minutes before he'd asked me to read a passage from *The Old Curiosity Shop*, in an effort to stimulate discussion. He was big on classroom participation and often frustrated at the lack of it. We might have been more willing if he'd been receptive to our ideas, if he didn't ridicule them when they failed to meet intellectual standards better suited to university students than nine and ten year olds. To make matters worse, he was in one of his moods that day. Always on the volatile side, he was capable of lashing out at any moment. But there were times, for reasons unknown to us, when he was positively dangerous. I was not the first student he'd called on who had delved insufficiently into the meaning of the text. Earlier, he'd struck Holvag, who still had his head on his desk, whimpering into his folded arms. So I had good reason to be nervous. And yet, Wittgenstein had never laid a hand on me. I had always felt exempt, special, and I was eager to demonstrate that specialness, to impress my difficult and brilliant schoolmaster while establishing once and for all my superiority over the rest of the class. I'd launched confidently into the reading of the assigned passage.

I'd been going along without the slightest hesitation when I came to a word that was unfamiliar to me. The word—I shall never forget it—was "abnegations." My vocabulary was better than average, easily the best in the class, but this was a new word for me. I couldn't even pronounce it, though I tried several times. When I decided to bypass it and read on, Wittgenstein stopped me, refusing to let me continue until I got it right.

"Abneg...abna..."

"No!"

I jumped. My face burned, my throat started to close up. Yet I tried again.

"No! No! No!" He was in a towering rage. I use that hackneyed phrase because his fury seemed to have added several inches to his diminutive stature. His contorted visage loomed above me. I knew something horrible was coming. I could almost see his mind working, a mind considered by many to be one of the most subtle and profound of the twentieth century. His blue eyes shifted in their deep sockets as he tried to fix on the condign punishment for this particular idiocy. He turned sharply and marched to the front of the classroom. He grabbed the yardstick he kept beside his desk and strode back down the aisle. Before I knew what was happening, before I could think to protect myself, he raised the yardstick and brought it down on top of my head.

Eva was more dear to me than life itself, but after fifteen years of marriage, we both knew the value of spending time apart, of pursuing interests independent of the other. While on Sunday nights Eva socialized with friends, I, the introvert in the marriage, preferred to devote myself to solitary endeavors. I treasured these few hours alone and enjoyed planning in advance how I would spend them. I had already decided that, while grading papers, I would listen to my Budapest String Quartet recordings of Beethoven's late quartets. Eva was partial to the early and middle quartets, but found the late ones, with their sometimes noisy dissonance, hard to take. It was a chance to hear them without worrying about their effect on Eva's nerves, either to lie on the couch and listen with my eyes closed, or to increase the volume and dance around the room.

It was nightfall. I flipped on the lights in the living room, arranged myself in my favorite chair, and began reading my students' essays. I was only half way through the first one when my concentration faltered. I couldn't relax, I couldn't think, knowing he was probably still out there. I stepped into the darkened bedroom so I could peek through the blinds undetected. There he was, cane in hand, clearly visible thanks to a nearly full moon and his light-colored clothing.

I went back to the living room, determined to get down to work. I disliked grading papers as much as the next teacher, and sometimes, in order to focus my attention, I would read them aloud. I tried this, almost shouting at one point, but it was no use. A distance of two decades had not sufficed to help me forget one of the most traumatic events of my childhood. What made me think I could erase it from my consciousness now, when its perpetrator was only fifty feet from my door? After a few more failed attempts to immerse myself in my work, and just as many trips to the bedroom to monitor Wittgenstein's movements (he had not budged), I became extremely agitated. Who did he think he was, staking out my home as if I were some criminal? I almost hoped he'd cross my property line so that I could call the authorities.

I'd lived in Trattenburg my whole life. A citizen in good standing, a fixture in the community, I was on a first name basis with members of the police department. One word from me and I could have had him arrested on vagrancy charges. The drawback there, however, was that I might be legally obligated to appear with him before the magistrate. It might bring me face to face with him, and I was determined to deny him that opportunity. And something else. I was afraid. Not even Eva seemed to understand that. I was no longer the scrawny, tow-haired child who, following the yardstick incident, shook with fear whenever I entered Herr Wittgenstein's classroom, my anticipation of another assault so great (to this day I have a stronger than normal startle response), that my schoolwork began to suffer and I barely managed to be promoted to the next grade. I was all grown up now, a good four inches taller and fifty pounds heavier than the aging little man standing outside my house, but deep down there still existed that frightened schoolboy who was always waiting for the next blow. I would do whatever it took to protect him.

Perhaps Wittgenstein had grown weary of his vigil and decided to make his move before losing his resolve, or perhaps he was just cold. Whatever the reason, he picked a moment just after nine o'clock to call out in a loud, clear voice,

"Konrad. Konrad Kliberg."

It so happened I was peering through the blinds just then. I stepped back from the window and pressed myself against the wall, like an escaped convict making a last stand in an abandoned house.

"Konrad. Let me in."

There was a different quality to his voice and I realized he'd moved closer to the house. A quick peek confirmed that he now stood at the edge of the lawn, in a direct line with the front door.

"Konrad. Open up. I need to talk to you."

He needed to talk to me. It was always about him.

In the living room, I shook out of its sleeve Quartet no. 15 in A minor, the fifth movement, allegro appassionato. I put it on the record player and turned up the volume.

As loud as it was, I practically leapt from my chair when the knocking started, the repeated thud of fist against wood. I ignored this. Then came a sharp rapping noise. He was beating on the door with his cane.

I shouted over the music, "If you don't leave my property this instant, I'm calling the police. They're friends of mine."

The rapping stopped. He wasn't so far gone he couldn't respond rationally to a threat, I decided. Then I heard something in the bedroom, a scraping sound. I ran in, gently lifted one of the blinds and peered out. Wittgenstein's shadowy figure was standing amid the hedges. He was trying to insert the tip of his cane at the base of the window in a desperate effort to pry it open. When that failed, he tried the same thing along the sides. Suddenly he dashed from sight. He was surprisingly agile and fleet of foot, for a man his age. I stood in the middle of the bedroom with my fists clenched, my heart thudding, wondering where and when he would strike next. I heard something at the back of the house and ran down the hall to the kitchen. He was applying his cane to the window above the sink in the same absurd fashion.

"All the windows are locked, you fool!"

He ducked from sight. Seconds later the kitchen doorknob began to jiggle. I laughed out loud. There were two strong locks on the door. He could have jiggled the knob all night without gaining access. I breathed a little easier. The muscles in my back and legs, relaxing after hours of sustained tension, ached. All at once there was a terrific crash. Wittgenstein had used his walking stick to shatter the glass panel closest to the door knob. He jabbed again and again at the window, sending shards skittering across the tiles. I watched in horror as his little hand snaked through the opening he'd created, his fingers working deftly at the locks, then turning the knob. The door opened.

I rushed over and pressed my weight against my side of the door. I was by no means a weakling, but I could not get the door to shut. Wittgenstein, a veteran of the Great War, a man of Spartan personal habits, and a fanatical walker, was not lacking in physical strength.

"I must talk to you," he said.

"Never."

Despite my efforts, he got his foot inside the kitchen, then all of one arm, then part of a leg. He was able to gain a bit of traction on the cement patio, while I was in my stockinged feet and slipping constantly on the slick tiles. As hard as I tried, I could not overcome this disadvantage.

I fled the kitchen and ran into the living room. I was a man seeking refuge inside his own home.

I spun around. Wittgenstein was standing at the other end of the hallway in semi-darkness. His body was in silhouette, legs apart, shoulders squared, hair sticking straight up. I couldn't see his face but I could feel his intense gaze, the one that years before was a prelude to some brutal act. He started down the hall, swinging his cane, his shoes crunching glass. I snatched up a lamp and threw it at him. It fell short of his advancing figure. I reached for the nearest large object, my reading chair. Made of mahogany, it must have weighed thirty pounds, but the adrenalin was flowing and I raised it above my head as if it were cardboard. Wittgenstein halted just inside the living room. We stared at each other. He was only one or two small steps away from crossing an invisible line, my threshold of safety. He must have seen that I was fully capable of preventing him from taking those last steps, that my intentions were serious, because he began slowly backing up. I was moving toward him when I heard the key turning in the lock.

It was Eva. She stood aghast in the doorway, taking in the bizarre tableau.

"He broke in," I said. "I couldn't stop him."

The record player, blaring Beethoven's frenzied music, was to Eva's immediate left. She switched it off.

The chair was suddenly insupportable, my arms quivering under its weight. Eva hurried over and helped me lower it to the floor. I collapsed into it. She gasped.

"Your feet," she said.

The bottoms of my socks were red with blood. I hadn't realized I'd been walking on shards.

She looked at Wittgenstein. "What have you done to my husband?"

Before he could speak, she stripped the socks off my feet, ran to the bathroom and came back with some dampened towels. She was crying as she picked the bits of glass out of my feet and dabbed at the wounds. I flinched during these ministrations but managed not to cry out. Wittgenstein, meanwhile, had neither moved nor spoken.

Eva wrapped a towel around each foot, dragged over the ottoman and gingerly elevated them. She stood, dried her eyes on her sleeve and walked over to Wittgenstein. She got right in his face.

"Get out of our house."

I didn't know what to expect. He watched her impassively, yet I could see the muscles working in his angular jaw, the knuckles of his tiny hand whitening as he squeezed the handle of his walking stick.

"Get out," she said, more quietly but with undiminished force.

Wittgenstein still hesitated, as if he were trying to make up his mind about something. I actually felt pity for him in that moment. He seemed so tortured, so driven, so helplessly who he was. At last he lowered his eyes and stepped around Eva, heading for the door. He had his hand on the knob when he turned and looked at me.

"I'm sorry," he said. He gave a quick little bow and left. I listened to the rat-tat-tatting of his cane as he retreated from the house. I could still hear it when Eva went over and closed the door. I hear it to this day.

Mercy

W hen I got home that night there was an angel in my apartment. He (she?) was sitting on the end of the sofa and flipping through the latest *Harper's*. Closing the magazine, the angel looked up and smiled: blazing white teeth above a heart-shaped chin. I'd never gone in for the androgynous type, but even I could see what a dazzling creature this was: the wavy blond hair; the large blue eyes almost too far apart; the beautiful long legs. If this was typical of angels, they were certainly a good looking bunch.

I was about to ask what she (to make a choice) was doing here when I thought how rude that would sound, as it might to inquire of anyone in the first moments of an unexpected visit their purpose for dropping in. Instead I said, "Is there anything I can get you?"

She considered this. "A drink would be nice." Her voice was in the medium range.

"Ginger ale, orange juice, Pepsi..."

"Have you anything alcoholic?"

I described the contents of my liquor cabinet.

"I'd love a sherry."

In the kitchen, I got down some glasses and fixed the drinks, mine a double Wild Turkey with a splash of seltzer. I needed it after the evening I'd had. I opened a can of cashew halves and poured them into a bowl. I'd gone shopping yesterday and the cupboards were filled with goodies. I'd also cleaned the apartment from top to bottom. I now saw all my preparations for what they were: absurd, and not a little pathetic. But at least the place had been made suitable for surprise guests.

The angel held the serving tray for me while I cleared space on the coffee table, stacking all the high-toned books and magazines I'd scattered about to suggest the elevated character of my leisure hours. Pretentious idiot! She placed the tray on the table and then lifted the glass of sherry by the tips of her tapered fingers; not in an overly-delicate way, but neither was it done without delicacy. At her suggestion, we clinked glasses. She was a couple of inches shorter than I was, with a narrow waist, elegantly sloping shoulders and a nicely shaped behind. Her white clingy robe, more like a form-fitting toga, showed off her body to excellent effect.

"Like what you see?" she asked.

I was embarrassed by the question and tried to ignore it.

"You're shy," she said. "I like that." Eyeing me over the rim of her glass, she took a sip. "Amontillado?"

"That's right."

"It's delicious."

I scooped up some cashews.

Seated now, she patted the cushion next to her. I backed into the chair on the opposite side of the room.

"I'm sorry things didn't go as you'd hoped this evening," she said.

Angels are all-knowing, I understood. It made me uncomfortable to think she would know about the newly purchased lambskin condoms in the night table beside my bed. And there were all the back issues of *Playboy* and *Penthouse* and, most ashamedly, the two extremely expensive issues of *Beaver Watch*, hidden away in the bottom of the hall closet. It struck me, too, that my omniscient visitor must have known what type of sherry she'd been served, and I wondered if a little vanity wasn't characteristic of angels.

She added sweetly, "I do wish it had gone differently."

"Thank you," I said. "That's very kind."

I had tried everything else I could think of to meet women—bar hopping, personal ads, walking up and introducing myself in supermarkets (the least effective)—so why not dance lessons? At forty-nine, with most of your hair gone, and all of your muscle tone, with the evidence piling up that you are no longer a "catch," you tell yourself it may be time to call it quits, in the amatory department. But then it begins to prey on you that you will never add to your storehouse of sexual memories, that those four women you slept with (only four!) will be it. You realize that those magazines are *just not enough.*

There were twenty of us in the class. We met every Thursday at 6:15 at the Community Center, each of the twelve lessons devoted to a different dance step. I spotted her the first night, polka night. She was slim-hipped yet voluptuous in a Fifties, Joi Lansing sort of way. I asked her if she'd consent to be my partner. She declined, saying she'd promised herself to another. But the next Thursday I was sure I saw her glancing over her partner's shoulder at me, as if she'd come to regret her choice. I decided to wait until tonight, the night of the final lesson, before giving her another chance. I did not want to appear too eager, always a problem for me in the past; also, perhaps, I wanted her to suffer just a little. In what seemed the work of providence, both her and my regular partner did not show up for class. Thrown together, as it were, we danced the tango for the next two hours. She was, I noted, aloof and taciturn throughout the lesson, but I interpreted this as her being true to the spirit of that smoldering, teasing, quintessentially romantic dance.

After class, I caught up with her in the poorly lit parking lot. As she was pulling on her gloves, both of us still a little breathless from our dance floor exertions, I said, repeating the sentences I'd been rehearsing for weeks, "Would you like to go for a cup of coffee? It's only eight-thirty."

"No, thank you," she said, inserting the key in her car door. "I have to meet friends."

"Well, would it be okay if I called you some time?"

"No."

"I'm sorry?"

"I'd prefer you didn't call. You're blocking the door."

I hadn't realized I was standing in the way and moved aside. Then I did something I shouldn't have, but that seemed natural after a night of close physical proximity. I reached out and took hold of her arm. She shook my hand off and began digging in her purse. She yanked out something white and cylindrical and pointed it at my eyes. "Don't make me use this."

"Whoa," I said. "You've got me all wrong. I'm not like that." I stepped closer. "When do you think you'll be through with your friends?"

She took aim and sprayed.

The angel compressed her lips into a sympathetic smile. "I am sorry."

"The experience isn't a total loss," I said. "You never know when the cha-cha's going to come back in."

She did not laugh. And for that I was grateful. What I needed more than anything right then was for someone, or something, to take my pain seriously.

"Are you my guardian angel?"

"Everyone asks that. No. Let's just say I'm an angel of mercy. I've taken pity on you."

"I don't want pity."

"Of course you do. Everybody wants pity."

I thought about that. "Is that why you're here? To pity me?

"Yes. And to succor you. I've come to give you succor." She broke into titters. "It's been a long time, has it not, since you were last succored?"

My face reddened. This angel could be surprisingly childish.

Composing herself, she said in a different tone, "I hope you'll rethink your decision."

"What decision?"

"The one you made this evening."

On the drive home, my eyes still smarting (I'd staggered around the parking lot until I located the entrance to the Community Center in whose bathroom I splashed into my inflamed sockets handful after handful of cold water), I'd vowed total celibacy from that day forward. I no longer knew how to be with a woman; that much was clear. I had turned into some sort of ogre. From now on I would content myself with sublimations and substitutes. I would spend my nights in. "Why should I?"

"It's too rash, too absolute, for someone your age—any age. You never know what will happen." She turned off the table lamp. "How about some music? Do you have any Enya?"

She knew I did, of course. I put the disk in the CD player.

She closed her eyes and waved a hand through the air. "I love this, don't you?"

We listened to the music for a while. The only light came from the kitchen, casting the angel in a flattering chiaroscuro glow. It had the effect of softening her features, rounding off her somewhat angular jaw, plumping her lips to a vampish pout, hooding the eyes to the point of salaciousness. I found myself staring. Returning my gaze, she tucked her chin *a la* Lauren Bacall, loose strands of that golden mane falling over the side of her face, partially obscuring one eye. She smiled, her mouth curling up at one corner. "Why don't you come over here next to me?"

How often had I dreamed about some beautiful young woman throwing herself at me? It was probably my most potent erotic fantasy. That wasn't quite what this was, yet I was still tempted. And I had always had a thing for blondes.

Shamelessly, she reached down and pulled the hem of her robe above her knees and slowly crossed them. She gave her head a shake. "Oh, come on. I won't bite—*hard*."

I felt my blood jump.

She rose from the sofa and, striding over, her sandals lightly flip-flopping, took my hand and pulled me gently out of my chair. She led me down the hall and into the bedroom. We sat side by side on the edge of the bed, our thighs touching. "This is much better, isn't it?"

She opened the drawer of the night table and took out the red candle and the box of kitchen matches I'd put there earlier. The tiny flame projected our shadows over the wall and ceiling. She returned the matches to the drawer, leaned close and stroked my head, her fingers passing easily through my thinning hair, but—and this was her genius—it was as if she preferred my head of hair to all others, as if she would rather run her fingers through my vanishing tresses than the most luxuriant in the world.

"I'm not very good," I said.

"That's all right. I am."

"I'm totally out of practice."

"Shut up," the angel said, "and kiss me."

I normally restrict myself to two bourbons per night, but I had made myself a generous third, and then a fourth. I'd turned up the volume on the CD player, enough to drown out all the crying. Even so, the occasional sob got through. I kept recalling that wrenching moment in *Peter Pan* when Mary Martin returns to the earthly bedroom where it all began and is confronted with the fact that the children she/he took to Never Never Land so long ago have betrayed her/him—that is, they've grown up. Peter falls to the floor and weeps. The poignancy is almost unbearable. It's finally alleviated when Wendy's daughter wakes up—"Boy? Why are you crying?"—and allows herself to be whisked off to Never Never Land. For a while. You know she'll want to return eventually, just like her mother, just like everyone, continuing, for Peter, the endless cycle of rejection and abandonment.

I went down the hall and stood in the doorway. The angel was just where I'd left her, curled up on the far side of the bed, facing the wall. You would have thought she was asleep if not for the sniffling and nose blowing.

"I'm sorry," I said for the hundredth time.

She did not respond.

I'd known from those first passionate, sherry-flavored kisses, that I was under the spell of a creature of exceptional skill and sensitivity. She kissed me as I'd always wanted to be kissed, held me as I'd always wanted to be held. Occasionally she interrupted these attentions to whisper sweet nothings—though not too sweet. There was nothing dirty about them; more like borderline bad taste. In other words, just what one wants in that situation. She started playing with the back of my neck, massaging it, grazing it with her fingertips, something I liked enormously, my own personal erogenous zone. I was soon in a state of extreme arousal. If only we had stopped there! But already her hand had begun to roam. I felt it on my leg, my knee, sliding up my thigh. It was at this point my senses went on red alert. I saw the thickish wrists, the veined forearms, the underdeveloped chest area. I heard the timbre in her voice. I felt against my skin the short bristly hairs of an incipient mustache. I stayed the angel's hand.

Wounded, she turned on me her big blue eyes, wet with tears.

"It's not you," I said. "It's me."

"You don't like me." It was not a question.

"Of course I like you."

"You don't like me—in that way."

"I do. I mean…it's complicated."

"You don't want me. There's nothing complicated about that."

I did my best to comfort her. She wouldn't have it. *"Don't you touch me. Don't you dare."*

Now I fetched some tissues and reentered the bedroom. She refused to take them, though I did manage to get her to turn away from the wall. Pouting, she pressed her back against the headboard.

"Feeling better?" I said.

No answer.

I dabbed at her cheeks with the tissues. "I'm sure it would have been great. *You're* great."

She sniffled.

"I know I'll regret it some day. I regret it now."

"I only wanted to please you."

"You have. You're not what I'm used to, that's all. Try not to take it so personally."

More long faces.

"I wish there were some way I could make it up to you."

"It's too late for that."

"Give me your hand."

"No."

"Let me have your hand."

"Aren't you afraid of getting my cooties?"

I pried her hand lose from her forearm and held it. Had she never experienced rejection before, I wondered? Or had she, like Peter, experienced it all too often?"

We sat like that for some time, holding hands, the guttering candle bouncing our shadows around the room, the oceanic music in the background.

"Do you know what I'm thinking?" I said.

She shook her head.

"Yes, you do."

"Forget it."

I stood up, her hand still in mine.

"I'm not in the mood," she said.

I gave her arm a little tug. "Please."

She let me pull her to her feet. I placed my hand on her hip. Grudgingly, she followed my lead while keeping me at near arms-length, her face averted. We continued dancing for several minutes in that stilted fashion. Then I drew her to me. She didn't resist.

Putting her arms around me, she rested her head on my shoulder.

"I'm such a fool," she said.

"No, you're not."

We swayed side to side, shuffling around the bedroom. Eventually the music stopped. A little later the candle went out. We stood there without moving. After a while, we were just holding each other.

About the Author

John Picard, a native of Washington, D.C., lives in Greensboro, North Carolina. He earned his B.A. in English at the University of Maryland in 1973 and his MFA in creative writing from the University of North Carolina at Greensboro in 1989. He is currently an employee of UNCG's Jackson Library. Before moving to Greensboro he had many of  the jobs common to struggling writers: general office worker, hotel reservations clerk, chauffeur, courier, dish washer. He has published stories in the *Iowa Review*, for which he received the Tim McGinnis award for humorous fiction, *Greensboro Review*, *Mid-American Review*, *The Seattle Review*, and others. He is also a recipient of a North Carolina Arts Council grant for fiction.